BIBLIOGRAPHY

The principal source of information was the local
newspaper archive at the Blackpool Central Library.

Other sources:

The Grand Theatre archives

The Oxford Companion to the Theatre (OUP)

Who's Who in the Theatre (Pitman)

Daly's: Biography of a Theatre (W.H. Allen) by D. Forbes Winslow

Edwardian Popular Music (David & Charles) by Ronald Pearsall

Dames of the Theatre (W.H. Allen) by Eric Johns

ILLUSTRATIONS

Portraits: The author's collection of publicity photographs

Cover picture: The earliest known photo of the Grand, dated by the
poster as 1901 or 1902, taken from the 1910 Blackpool Guide

Other pictures: The Grand Theatre archives

ACKNOWLEDGEMENTS

The Editor of the Evening Gazette for permission to
quote from reviews and reports

The staff of the reference section at Blackpool Central
Library for their assistance

The Grand Theatre and the Friends of the Grand
for supporting this publication

INTRODUCTION

Blackpool's Grand Theatre is one hundred years old in 1994. It almost didn't make it. In 1972 it was scheduled for demolition as part of a town centre redevelopment area but was saved by the campaigning Friends of the Grand. Today it is one of the success stories of the British theatre, owned and managed by the Grand Theatre Trust Limited. It is our good fortune that the Grand has survived largely in the original Victorian splendour invested by its architect, Frank Matcham. From the opening month, the Grand has been known as 'Matcham's Masterpiece' – a title cleverly coined by Thomas Sergenson, the first owner of the theatre and master showman in the Victorian manner. It was Sergenson, above any other, who set the style and standard for which Blackpool entertainment became famous. This book is the first of two books celebrating the Grand's one hundred years. It covers the period to 1930, with emphasis on the stars and shows that appeared there. The second book, covering 1930 to the present day, will be published early in centenary year and will deal at greater length with names and events that are of more recent memory.

CONTENTS

Barry Band is a member of the Grand Theatre Trust Ltd., and since 1983 has been the Illuminations Fund Organiser for Blackpool Council. For 25 years he was a journalist on Lancashire newspapers. He was born in Blackpool in 1938 and attended Devonshire School and the old grammar school.

CHAPTER ONE

The People's Showman

HE last quarter of the 19th century in Blackpool was a period of extravagant development. A small bathing resort became the busiest holiday town in Britain. But the early promoters had a very different vision. They wanted Blackpool to be a select haven where middle class ladies and gentlemen could stroll in the clean promenade air during the day and enjoy orchestral concerts and operatic recitals in the evening. The dream started to go wrong in the late 1870s when increasing numbers of working class trippers poured in to the town's second rail terminal, which was just fifty yards from the sands on Central Beach.

The Victorian gentlemen promoters had little idea what kind of entertainment was wanted by the lower classes. It certainly wasn't classical music. It took a newcomer to the town, Thomas Sergenson, to hit on the formula that could make money although it was several years before the conservative Winter Gardens Company got the message.

Sergenson arrived from Preston in the mid-1870s and was employed in some managerial role at the public baths on Hygiene Terrace, on the promenade just south of Church Street. The site was earmarked by William Henry Cocker, and his Lane Ends Development Company, as the site of the Prince of Wales development, consisting of a theatre, public baths and a shopping arcade.

Cocker and his directors appointed Sergenson their treasurer and the building opened in 1879 at a cost of £60,000, well over budget. Britain was in the grip of an economic slump and business was dreadful. The first actor-manager to lease the theatre could not pay his way and the directors offered it to Sergenson. He declined. The following year another actor-manager gave up the task and the desperate directors again offered the hall to Sergenson. Their terms were irresistible. Sergenson would have a five-year lease with an option to renew and he would only pay a rental if he made a profit.

At the age of 27, with no obvious theatrical experience, Sergenson launched his career as the people's showman with a policy of low comedy, popular music and favourite melodramas, performed by touring companies on a weekly basis. Sergenson leased the theatre until 1897 when the company, having never paid a dividend, sold the site at a handsome profit to a company that was to build an even bigger white elephant, the theatre, circus and ballroom complex named the Alhambra. It went bankrupt in three years and was bought cheaply by the Blackpool Tower Company and reopened as the Palace. This theatre-cinema-ballroom complex closed in 1961 to make way for Lewis's department store, which went into liquidation in 1992, to be snapped up for retail redevelopment.

In the 1870s, the Winter Gardens and the Prince of Wales development had one thing in common: the chairman of both ventures was William Henry Cocker, first Mayor of Blackpool and one of the principal investors in the resort's 'grand dream'. His enthusiasm was not backed by commercial awareness and he died in poverty.

Sergenson must have been successful at the Prince of Wales Theatre because he was soon offered the lease of the Theatre Royal, in Talbot Square (in what is now the Yate's Wine Lodge block). The showman took over and applied his popular policy. So far he had not been called on to make any significant investment and was making a living out of the misfortunes of the Victorian gentlemen promoters and property owners.

In the early years of his career the young showman competed with, and often out-smarted, the important Winter Gardens Company, which must have dismayed William Henry Cocker, who had a foot in both camps. An example of the Sergenson flair for self-promotion came in August, 1882, after a performance at the Winter Gardens Pavilion by the legendary French actress Sarah Bernhardt. The Gardens directors were pursuing their policy of cultural edification and in this event they had a sell-out for the 'divine Sarah'.

However, the pavilion was not a conventional theatre. It was used for orchestral concerts and had shutters in the walls which could be opened to extend the viewing area to the horseshoe corridor which still runs around the Pavilion. So many people were clamouring to see the great tragedienne that the management raised the shutters and sold more tickets, for the company was in dire need of revenue.

Inevitably, there was a lot of background noise and the Pavilion's poor acoustics were made even worse. Few could hear the actress. Not that they were missing much because Bernhardt was performing Dumas's classic, *La Dame Aux Camelias* in French! There were shouts of 'speak up' and the actress, upset by the rowdy reception, walked off and returned to her suite at the Clifton Hotel. The Gardens company's prestigious event collapsed into chaos. The audience refused to accept an understudy and demanded their money back. In the confusion some scallywags smartly switched to more expensive areas and made a profit on the evening.

A few days later the Gazette-News printed a letter of explanation from the actress. She had been suffering from a sore throat and had been unable to continue the play. And the letter stated: 'If the directors had given the performance in the Prince of Wales Theatre they may have made less money but I could have played despite my suffering, sure of being heard and understood.' The letter concluded: 'Je suis une artiste et non une exhibition'.

It has been written that Thomas Sergenson heard about the letter on the night before publication and rushed round to his printer's home to arrange for large posters to be displayed around town, highlighting Sarah Bernhardt's praise for the Prince of Wales Theatre. (One of the posters actually appeared on a billboard opposite the Winter Gardens!)

This does not explain how the imperious French actress, on a one-night engagement in Blackpool, could have become so familiar with the qualities of Sergenson's rented theatre! Could the canny Sergenson actually have engineered the letter on behalf of the actress, affording her an apology to the town and giving his printer time to prepare the posters?

Sergenson was apparently making good profits from his two rented theatres and from other ventures. Local newspaper items indicated he had three or four touring companies and, for an unknown period, the lease of the Princes Theatre, Bradford.

In 1887 he was prosperous enough to lead a small consortium in the purchase of a row of old cottages and shops at the corner of Church Street and St Ann Street (now Corporation Street), a strategic site midway between the Promenade and the Winter Gardens. Sergenson's aim was to build a modern theatre with the comfort and capacity his little rented theatres could not provide.

A sign went up stating that work would start on 'the Grand Theatre and Opera House' in November, 1888. Sergenson thought that by having five shops on the Church Street frontage, he would be able to trade successfully. But for once his promotional flair rebounded. His plan was the last straw for the ailing Winter Gardens Company. After a poor season and with no manager, the directors could envisage lone wolf Sergenson becoming the resort's largest entertainment operator.

Within weeks the Gardens directors, with W.H. Cocker still chairman, had appointed a new general manager in William Holland, a London music hall showman who had just lost a fortune on a theatrical flop. His style and experience were exactly what the Gardens needed and it was the first truly commercial decision that the directors had made in ten years. Holland soon assessed the Pavilion as unsuitable for stage shows and told the board that they needed a proper theatre. His views coincided with a faction of directors who had been arguing the same case against the wishes of Cocker and his group.

The battle led to a boardroom split and the chairman's resignation in June, 1888. At the same time, Sergenson announced that plans for the Grand were ready and his first architect, William Longley, of Bradford, was calling for tenders. The Winter Gardens Company responded by asking architect Frank Matcham (who was later to design the Grand) to give them an Opera House as soon as possible. Sergenson took the cautious course and did not get involved in the race.

If the Gardens directors thought they had beaten their rival, they were mistaken. Sergenson built his Church Street shops and, a month after the Opera House opened with the D'Oyly Carte Opera Company in June, 1889, he launched *The Grand Circus* on his back lot, engaging Ohmy's Circus for the first season. 'Ohmy' was a noted aerial artist called Joe Smith, whose exploits made the crowds gasp 'Oh my'.

The site bought by Thomas Sergenson in 1887 for the Grand Theatre.

Sergenson booked a different circus each year for his wood and iron 'big top' and claimed in a newspaper ad that 87,000 had seen the circus in a year. It put paid to *Newsome's Circus,* a long-time summer tenant on the Winter Gardens' spare land and the Gardens directors lost their £1,000 annual rental.

Sergenson was twice in trouble for breaking building by-laws but it could not have been too serious for he was elected a Conservative councillor in 1890 and a year later was made chairman of the Advertising Committee, forerunner of today's Tourism Committee.

He watched the progress on the Blackpool Tower project, with its purpose-built circus, and closed his circus 'shed' in mid-September, 1893. Work began immediately on Frank Matcham's magnificent Grand Theatre to Sergenson's brief of 'The best, prettiest and cosiest theatre possible.' Incredibly, it took just nine months and cost £20,000 — a fortune in those days. The Grand opened on July 23, 1894, two months after the Tower. Even before the opening, Sergenson had dubbed it 'Matcham's Masterpiece' and the Press duly adopted the description.

Sergenson had steadily improved his shows at the Prince of Wales Theatre and had presented big names like George Alexander, Edward Compton, Edward Terry, Dorothy Baird and Isobel Bateman. But for his impressive opening season at the Grand he needed many more top-liners, particularly on the musical side.

Boldly, he went to the most famous names and secured the leading touring opera company, the top light musical show of the year, two premier comedy companies and two of the leading actors of the day.

The two brilliant men who made the Grand: architect Frank Matcham (left) and showman Thomas Sergenson.

For the opening week he signed actor-manager Wilson Barrett to give four plays, beginning with *Hamlet*. He had often appeared at the Opera House and may not have been Sergenson's first choice. There is nothing on record but it would have been the proprietor's style to attempt a 'first time in Blackpool' attraction for the new theatre.

First on his list could have been Henry Irving but he had London commitments after a long American tour. Second could have been Beerbohm Tree, who agreed to do a September week at the Grand. Wilson Barrett was an assured local attraction but it does seem less than triumphant that Sergenson actually preferred him for the Grand's opening in the same repertoire of plays that Barrett had twice done at the Opera House!

In a Press interview Barrett said he first visited Blackpool in 1863, when he was seventeen, with a stock company that played a season at a place he called 'the old Theatre Royal' on the promenade but he could not give its exact location. He said he often appeared with his late wife, Miss Heath, under Sergenson's management at the new Theatre Royal in the 1880s, before switching to the new Opera House.

On the Friday before the Grand's opening, the papers reported a hive of activity at the beautiful new building on Church Street, with workmen racing to complete the job. Delays would have cost Sergenson a fortune in guarantees to the visiting companies but luck — which stayed with him through three decades of Blackpool's risky, formative years — held true.

On Monday, July 23, 1894, the cream of the area's civic and business life, including other entertainment managers, were present in the flower-decked theatre. The champagne flowed. Even the programmes were printed on silk and perfumed. Nobility was respresented by Lady Queensbury and her party.

Thomas Sergenson's Grand Dream had come true.

CHAPTER TWO
'Matcham's Masterpiece'

IN 1972, when the Grand Theatre site was being measured by the developers for a concrete overcoat, few people had heard of Frank Matcham. Today he is recognised as a theatre architect of extraordinary talent. His surviving theatres have been restored and reopened. Books have been published on his work.

Since the mid-1970s, major Matcham theatres to be restored and reopened include the Theatre Royal, Nottingham, the Opera House, Buxton, the Grand Opera House, Belfast, and the Lyric, Hammersmith.

In the case of Blackpool's Grand Theatre, there is no doubt that Matcham's functional and compact design, allied to beautiful plasterwork and decoration, was an important 'plus' factor in the saving of the theatre from demolition in 1972.

The Grand is a perfect example of Matcham's ability to design a large seating capacity into a small auditorium and also of his skill in tackling odd-shaped sites; at the Grand it was an L-shape to fit round a block of shops.

Artistes who have played the Grand are unanimous in their praise of the acoustics and the intimate atmosphere. Audiences join them in agreeing that the theatre is an absolute gem.

Matcham was born in 1854 at Newton Abbott, Devon, and joined the London office of J.T. Robinson, the Lord Chamberlain's theatre consultant, in 1875. Three years later he married Robinson's daughter, Effie, but within a year his father-in-law died and Matcham took over a large architectural practice at the age of only 23. By the end of the century almost every town of note had a Matcham theatre or hall. His output was remarkable — ninety-two new theatres and more than fifty rebuilds, as well as halls and ballrooms, in a career spanning forty years. Matcham died in 1920.

His work in 1894 included the Grand Theatre, the Tower Ballroom, Blackpool, and five other theatre completions — the Bolton Grand, the Birmingham Empire, the Wakefield Opera House, the Belfast Grand Opera House and the Brixton Theatre.

Five years earlier he had designed the first Blackpool Opera House, and he was commissioned by the Blackpool Tower Company on various projects in the early years of the 20th Century. These included the remodelling of parts of the bankrupt Alhambra, which was bought by the Tower Company in 1903 and reopened as the Palace.

As well as his dozens of provincial theatres, Matcham designed several larger

London theatres including the 4,000 seat Hippodrome (now a disco), the Palladium, the Victoria Palace and the London Coliseum.

Matcham was a pioneer in the use of steel-work and the cantilever principle of supporting balconies and set new standards in theatre ventilation and safety measures.

His interest in the use of fibrous plaster techniques resulted in ornate interiors like the Grand's which is one of the few surviving examples of his genius.

How the theatre was described in the local Press

Report from the 'Blackpool Gazette and News', July 24, 1894

BLACKPOOL may now justifiably boast that no other watering place in the world offers such facilities for the recreation and enjoyment of its visitors. But it is not very many years since Blackpool was entirely dependent upon what may be described as itinerant entertainers for the amusement of its summer visitors. But we have now got very far beyond that stage, and we may already claim that for at least three months of the year no place in the kingdom, and we will not even except London, can offer the sight-seer so much for so small an expenditure of the current coin of the realm. Yesterday, another was added to the long list of Blackpool's places of resort, and Mr Thos. Sergenson, who has long been a spirited entrepreneur for the visiting masses, must be very heartily congratulated upon the enterprise which has its consummation in the New Grand Theatre and Opera House — admitted on all hands to be undoubtedly one of the finest theatres in the provinces.

Mr Frank Matcham, the well-known theatrical architect of 9 Warwick Court, London, was in the first instance given carte blanche, and a result of his labours there can be no question that the new Grand Theatre is about as near perfection as architectural skill can make it, and well deserves the title of 'Matcham's Masterpiece'.

The circular entrance at the corner of Church Street is a particularly fine example of stonework, and the dome and minaret cannot fail to attract the interested attention of all passing by. The entrance hall is prettily finished off with decorative ferneries and rockeries, while a handsome marble staircase leads to the dress circle and boxes, of which there are eight in number.

Entrance to the stalls is gained by a passage leading direct from the hall, and the seats, which close up automatically immediately the spectator rises, are upholstered in blue English velvet. The great width of the theatre finds room for a most spacious pit, and upon the parquetted floor there must be sitting room for at least a thousand persons. The dress circle is certain to be a most popular part of the house. The upholstered tip-up seats provide for about a hundred and sixty, and behind there is a spacious saloon, charmingly decorated, together with a promenade which will provide standing room for many more. The upper circle will easily seat from four hundred to five hundred, and here again the upholstery is in accord with the other parts of the house.

The gallery will provide accommodation for at least one thousand, the view of the stage from every part being uninterrupted, so that not far short of three thousand persons may witness the performance at one time all seated. There are handsome crushrooms, foyers and saloons, all parts of the house having separate retiring rooms, comfortably furnished and fitted with every convenience. The sanitary arrangements and ventilation are up to date in every particular, and special attention has been paid to the heating apparatus, by which the whole building can be warmed to any extent in winter. Hydrant and fittings for protection from fire are placed in convenient positions, while the electric light has been installed throughout. The fact that there are no columns to obstruct the view in any part of the house is a splendid feature of the building, and is accounted for by the fact that the framework, which is entirely of steel and of immense strength, is on the cantilever principle.

The stage is a large one, and capable of staging any of the largest operas or dramas 'on the road'. Large scene docks, property rooms, etc., are arranged in conjunction. Special attention has been given to the dressing-rooms; these are large, well arranged, and ventilated, comfortably furnished, heated and fitted with enamelled slate tables; lavatories with hot and cold water laid on. Retiring rooms, with bath and every convenience, are also provided, and these rooms are so placed that the artistes can make their entrance without crossing the stage. We have not yet referred to the decoration of the ceiling, the fine proscenium or the fronts of the dress circle or upper circle tiers which are all of a particular chaste and elegant character.

Encircling the proscenium arch are twelve small floral panels representing the months of the year. The background is cream, but gold is lavishly used, and blue — which is the prevailing colour throughout the theatre — is introduced with charming effect. At either side there are two magnificently painted panels which do the artist every credit. The ceiling also is divided into panels radiating from the fine centre piece from which hang the magnificent brass electroliers, and upon these panels are inscribed in letters of gold the names of famous composers, including Sullivan, Lecocq, Collier, Soloman, Herve, Offenbach etc. Cream and gold are also predominant colours in the beautiful plasterwork encircling the fronts of the upper tiers, while these are also relieved by prettily painted panels. The appearance of the stage front from any part of the house is most beautiful and the Grand deserves to rank as one of the handsomest theatres in the provinces, and we do not doubt that both residents and visitors will make haste to speedily see it for themselves.

The Opening Night

Report from the 'Blackpool Gazette and News', July 24, 1894

Mr Sergenson's decision to open the new Grand Theatre with Shakespeare, whom we may call the patron saint of the drama, must commend itself to all. Many managers have found that Shakespeare spells ruin, but that is of course when the doses are too big. We take it as an earnest of the manner in which Mr Sergenson intends to conduct his new venture that he should elect to produce 'Hamlet' — the masterpiece of the greatest playwright who ever lived — on the opening night. It was but fitting, therefore, that there should be a large and representative attendance last evening; the stalls, grand circle and boxes all being filled, there being but standing room in the pit, while the extensive seating accommodation in the upper circle and gallery were also well taken up. Evening dress was general in the stalls, circle and boxes, and the scene presented at the rising of the curtain was a very brilliant one indeed.

There were loud cries for a speech after the curtain had fallen, and Mr Wilson Barrett complied with the request upon his third appearance. He said:

"*Ladies and Gentlemen.*

"*You have been good enough to ask for a speech from me, and I must congratulate Blackpool most heartily upon the acquisition of this most beautiful temple of the drama. It is a matter of congratulation to Blackpool to the lessee, Mr Sergenson, and certainly to the architect, Mr Matcham, who designed it. (Hear, hear). In the first place, a theatre above all other places should be one in which the audience can see the stage and hear the actors. Ladies and gentlemen, I think that applies to this building, and I must say, seriously, that I have never yet spoken in any theatre with more ease and comfort than in this building tonight. It is not always the best designed theatre that achieves that very important result. As an actor devoted to his art I perhaps rather overstep what you may consider the bounds of discretion when I say that the erection of such a building as this in your town is a benefit not only to the town itself, but to every member of the community.*

"*There is a story told of the late Prince Albert, our good Queen's Consort, that when he went to Leeds he asked the then Mayor, 'What is the status of drama in your city,' and the Mayor said, 'Well, we don't think much of drama here.' 'Oh,' said the Prince, 'I am sorry to hear that, because I always measure the intellect of a community by the status of the drama in its midst.' It was a very apt reply, and one which bears* consideration, and upon that consideration you will find it perfectly true. (Applause).

"Amusement the public will have in this busy work-a-day world, when we are all toiling and struggling to occupy a foremost place, or a place where we can be respected. We must have some relaxation, and it is well when that relaxation is that which honest and honourable men can use without feeling that they are assisting at something which has a tendency to lower the morals of the people. (Applause). Most sincerely I congratulate this growing Blackpool – I do not know where it will extend to, but that is a matter time will show. I am not very old, but still I can remember when Blackpool had but one little theatre, and speaking from experience, the salaries were not great at that little theatre by any means. (Laughter). Had it not been, I am afraid to say, for the liberality of some of the little landladies at the not-then-very prosperous watering place, most of the actors would have had very small tables, and very little to put upon them to help them towards their arduous duties at night. I speak as one who knew and felt – and did not eat too much. (Laughter). But now I see you have your Tower, your theatres, gardens, palaces and I say with all my heart, 'Long may it improve as rapidly as it has done in the past.'

"Thousands upon thousands of people pour in to your town, and they must have amusement. Heaven knows, they deserve it, toiling the year through. It is a matter of congratulation to you, therefore, that you should have such a place as this in your midst. I thank you for your welcome home, for as some of you are aware, this is my first appearance in my own country after travelling thirty thousand miles in that great country beyond the ocean. I have brought my good company with me, and they are equally happy to be at home once more. And I hope we shall all endeavour to deserve some of the kindnesses you have showered upon us tonight."

Loud applause greeted the conclusion of the great actor's speech, vehement calls next arising for the appearance of Mr Sergenson and Mr Matcham. After a short delay, Mr Barrett once again appeared with Mr Matcham on his right and Mr Sergenson at his left, the trio merely bowing their acknowledgements. The theatre then rapidly cleared, the time having reached eleven-fifteen.

The silk programmes in honour of the first night were exquisitely perfumed with the new Tower Bouquet — a charming scent which Mr H.J. Kettlewell, of Church Street, Blackpool, has just introduced.

CHAPTER THREE

The Super Showman

T HE opening of the Grand Theatre placed Thomas Sergenson among the North's leading managers. The showman who had made his money from cheap and cheery comedy and melodramatic pot-boilers moved overnight into the Number One circuit of famous actors, spectacular musicals and high class opera, all of which were seen at the Grand in the first few weeks.

But if Sergenson's head was momentarily in rarified atmosphere, his feet were still on the ground. The week after Wilson Barrett gave his Hamlet on the new stage, Sergenson was presenting the old crowd-pleaser *East Lynne* at the Prince of Wales Theatre, a convenient 200 yards from the Grand's stage door.

Blackpool was awed by the Grand — 'this magnificent theatre, erected at enormous expense' as Sergenson proclaimed in his advertising in the local Gazette and News, adding that it could truthfully be described as 'the handsomest, safest, most comfortable, largest and best appointed theatre in the town and, when seen, will instantaneously be stamped as THE THEATRE.' One in the eye for the rival Winter Gardens Company, owners of the five-year old Opera House!

Sergenson was on familiar ground. The master of the promotional slogan and the clever advertising ploy could now speak with sincerity. After all, his new theatre **was** the finest in town and his shows **were** from the top shelf.

In the following week's issue of the newspaper, his advertisement carried the line 'Described by the Press as the prettiest theatre in the kingdom' — a phrase which Sergenson himself had coined and fed to the local reporters, who would have been so dazzled by the place that they could not fail to agree.

Prices for the opening week were also the prices of 'premium' shows at the Grand for the next fifteen years! They were: Boxes £1 1s to £2 2s; stalls and grand circle 4s; upper circle 2s 6d; pit 1s 6d; gallery 6d. Lesser attractions had lower prices.

When Wilson Barrett stepped onto the stage as *Hamlet* on Monday, July 23, 1894, the crowded house rose and applauded for several minutes, reported the Gazette and News. When he was allowed to continue, 'the audience listened in hushed silence and the acoustic qualities of the theatre were such that the melancholy Dane's soliloquies were perfectly heard in every part of the house.'

Whether Shakespeare's prose was appreciated by more than a small percentage of the audience could not be recorded. This was an 'occasion' performance, for one night only. Thomas Sergenson was well aware that the Bard's words spelled box office doom in the provinces and he had contracted Barrett to present a popular repertoire for the remainder of the week — *Ben-My-Chree, Virginius* and *Claudian.*

In Barrett's company, Austin Melford played Claudius in *Hamlet* and Maud Jeffries played Ophelia and other leading female roles that week. The call boy and juvenile player was Melford's son, Austin junior, aged ten, who thus assumed a noteworthy position in the Grand Theatre story. He became the performer with the longest professional link with the Grand — a span of sixty years — appearing many times in plays and revues, as well as being the writer and producer of several shows that visited the theatre. His last acting credit at the Grand was in 1954, with Coral Browne and Hugh Williams in *Affairs of State.*

Barrett, freshly returned from his fourth American tour, used his curtain speech to praise the theatre and stress the importance of theatre in a town's cultural life. "I have never yet spoken in any theatre with more ease and comfort than in this building," he said.

It was exactly what Thomas Sergenson wanted to hear and he broke into superlatives for his advertising copy for the following week. 'Pronounced the most magnificent theatre in the country' ... 'Instantaneous and glorious success' ... 'Mr Wilson Barrett says it is the most perfect theatre he has ever performed in ' ... 'Everyone charmed with this magnificent temple of the drama' were some of Sergenson's boasts.

From that July week, Wilson Barrett appeared exclusively at the Grand when he visited Blackpool and Sergenson made similar links with several other leading figures, thereby giving the Grand the advantage over the Opera House. The reason was not entirely due to the prettiness of the theatre or to Sergenson's excellent management, which was often praised by visiting companies. It was due to the fact that the Grand was the largest theatre in Blackpool and could give a higher cash return at the box office.

The stated capacity at the time is still a cause of puzzlement. The local Press reported it as 3,000, which today seems hard to believe, even allowing for the crush of bodies in the pit area and the standing room on all four levels, which is not allowed under today's fire and safety regulations. But sixteen years later, when the Grand was bought by the Blackpool Tower Company, the Tower shareholders were also given the figure of 3,000, by their company secretary, Robert Parker. It is difficult to imagine how the early managers packed so many people into such a compact theatre, and at what discomfort. Today the seating capacity is 1,200.

The second show to appear at the new theatre in 1984 was *Morocco Bound,* a burlesque opera by Arthur Branscombe with music by Osmond Carr and lyrics by Adrian Ross. This form of 'opera' was highly popular, going even further than Gilbert and Sullivan in lampooning the social and political foibles of the day. Topicality was its strength.

THE SUPER SHOWMAN

For the third week Sergenson had the smash hit farce *Charley's Aunt,* by Brandon Thomas, which was still running at London's Globe Theatre after two years. Grand Theatre audiences saw W.S. Penley appearing with his own company. Penley, a young actor with an eye for advancement, had bought the rights to the play from Thomas in 1892 and persuaded a stockbroker friend to invest £500 — a tidy sum at the time — in a stage tour. It flopped but in a last bid to avert bankruptcy they presented it in London. It was a hit and in two years the backer made £30,000 from his investment and Penley made his name as a top actor-manager. In Blackpool, Penley's company appeared exclusively at the Grand Theatre.

Sergenson aimed to satisfy all tastes and for his fourth week he presented the Carl Rosa Opera Company in a repertoire of eight shows, including *Faust, Carmen* and *Tannhauser.* The following week saw the first of many visits by actress-manager May Finney, who was always billed as 'Miss Fortescue and her London Company.' Her roles nearly always included Lady Teazle in *The School For Scandal* and Kate Hardcastle in *She Stoops To Conquer.*

The sixth week in the story of the new theatre saw its second *Hamlet* in the person of the celebrated Herbert Beerbohm Tree. The visit was advertised by Sergenson as 'the most impressive engagement of the season' — which suggests that the manager would have preferred Beerbohm Tree to have opened the theatre, rather than Wilson Barrett. Two star *Hamlets* in six weeks was good going for any theatre but one *Hamlet* every not too often would, in future, be good enough for Sergenson. Tree had a repertoire of popular plays and saved *Hamlet* for the Saturday evening. In a curtain speech the actor said: 'I can assure you there are not many theatres in the provinces, or even London, either better appointed or better managed.' Sergenson must have loved that remark and soon included it in his Press advertisements.

The week starting September 3 was one of the most important in the eventful theatrical career of the Grand's owner-manager. He presented the sensation of the London season, the musical comedy *A Gaiety Girl,* with music by Sidney Jones and lyrics by Adrian Ross. It was produced by George Edwardes, who dominated the lighter side of the English musical theatre for twenty years with his shows at the Gaiety and Daly's Theatres. *A Gaiety Girl* has been named by some theatre historians as the first English musical comedy and with several other Edwardes shows of the Nineties it established the famous Gaiety Girls — the glamorous leading ladies and chorus girls who were courted by the nobility.

It did tremendous business at the Grand and Sergenson emerged with an agreement to have first choice of the Edwardes musicals when they toured. He could hardly have realised what a bonanza this was to be. It was surely a major factor in the profitability of the Grand and a drawback for the rival Opera House, where they had to wait until Edwardes leased his shows to lesser producers. And when shows were new, Edwardes quickly sent them on tour with Blackpool, as a number one venue, seeing West End hits within

The Grand's first Hamlet, Wilson Barrett, who gave the Theatre's first performance, on July 23, 1894.

Beerbohm Tree, the second actor to play Hamlet at the Grand, six weeks after Wilson Barrett.

a few months, often with major stars heading the lavishly dressed productions.

After a week's visit by another Edwardes production, the burlesque opera *Don Juan,* the programmes turned to comedy plays with the Edward Compton Comedy Company in repertoire, in the week beginning September 17. Compton went on record as saying that he had played every British theatre of importance and, without hesitation, he could state he had never played in a more commodius, prettier, better appointed or conducted theatre than the Grand. The phrase was repeated in the theatre's next advertisements. Three weeks before Compton's 1894 visit, his wife had ensured the name would live on with distinction by giving birth to a daughter, Fay. There was also a son who became just as famous as Fay Compton. He was the author Compton Mackenzie.

The theatre's autumn bookings included two more notable names, comedy actor Edward Terry, with his repertoire of comedy roles and an American actress named Minnie Palmer, who has some claim to fame in the history of musical comedy. She toured extensively in *My Sweetheart,* a 'musical comedy drama' that appears to hold a place as the first structured production in the genre that became musical comedy in the Nineties, except that it originated in New York in 1882 and arrived in London two years later. It made several visits to the Grand, with Miss Palmer as the heroine, over a ten-year period.

A major name missing from the superstar line-up of Sergenson's 1894 opening season was Kendal. He had engaged the famous light comedy actress Madge Kendal and her husband, W. H. Kendal, for a September week but the couple were touring America with such success that the tour had to be extended. Mr and Mrs Kendal, as they were always billed, made amends the following autumn and became regular visitors to the Grand Theatre.

After a five-week closure in which the decoration of the theatre was completed, Sergenson opened for Christmas with a box office winner, *The Silver King,* by Charles Dornton's Company by permission of Wilson Barrett, who owned and had popularised the play. Under Sergenson's management the Grand would seldom have pantomimes at Christmas. They would come in during January and February. There were no 'season shows' during his ownership and even two-week bookings were unusual. Sergenson would always have a period of winter closure, of varying length, but it was greatly extended after the Grand was purchased by the Blackpool Tower Company in 1909. Apart from the two festive weeks and the annual Blackpool children's pantomime, which started in 1911, the Tower Company closed the Grand for five winter months in the first few years of their ownership.

CHAPTER FOUR

Meeting the Challenge

After Sergenson's tremendous opening season he faced the challenge of consolidating the Grand's reputation through 1895. He had stern competition from the Winter Gardens Company, where general manager William Holland bolstered business at the Opera House by giving theatre patrons free admission to the Gardens complex. Holland died at the end of 1895. We can only imagine what kind of a break this was for Sergenson although he had beaten Holland in 1895 attractions by presenting four major plays of the time: Shaw's *Arms and the Man,* Wilde's *The Importance of Being Earnest,* and Pinero's *The Second Mrs Tanqueray* and *The Notorious Mrs Ebsmith.* Wilson Barrett made two visits; in August with the same repertoire as 1894 and at Christmas in his new worldwide dramatic success *The Sign of the Cross.* He appeared as Marcus Superbus, the Prefect of Rome, torn between loyalty to the state and sympathy for the persecuted Christians. The author-actor had just returned from an American tour in the play, winning outstanding notices. A New York reviewer stated: 'As author, actor and manager, Wilson Barrett has scored the success of his life.' Now his Grand appearance in the play was another Sergenson coup.

The Kendals made their delayed Blackpool debut in September, staging a number of comedies including *Prude's Progress,* an early success of Jerome K. Jerome. Comedy was apparently going to be a Grand Theatre speciality because Sergenson also brought back W.S. Penley in *Charley's Aunt,* the Compton Comedy Company and Edward Terry — plus Emma Hutchison's Criterion Comedy Company and J. Comyns Carr's Company.

In November the Grand's manager presented 'a special, important and expensive engagement' of the young impressionist Cissie Loftus, the daughter of music hall star Marie Loftus. Only four years earlier Cissie had been a pupil at Blackpool's Layton Hill Convent. Now she was being paid the salary of a Cabinet Minister, said a local newspaper review, which described Miss Loftus as 'a brilliant young mimic.' She was accompanied to Blackpool by her husband, playwright and journalist Justin Huntley McCarthy.

Musical shows did not make a strong appearance during the year. Apart from the return visit of *A Gaiety Girl* the only other high spot was the George Edwardes production of the comic opera *His Excellency,* one of W.S. Gilbert's successes after his split with Arthur Sullivan. On this show Gilbert had collaborated with composer Osmond Carr and one of the stars was Robert Courtneidge (father of Cicely) who was soon to become a successful producer of musical comedy and comic opera.

In 1896 it was 'same again' as far as the comedy celebrities were concerned but Sergenson now began to reap the benefit of his deal with George Edwardes. Three of the powerful producer's musical comedies did great business when they each played a week in the late summer. The Grand was one of the first provincial theatres to see the Daly's Theatre success *The Geisha,* which Edwardes and his writers had tailored to suit the English liking for things Oriental, thanks to Gilbert and Sullivan's *The Mikado.* Marie Studholme played the title part created by Marie Tempest only six months earlier, and the male lead was Rutland Barrington, who had often played Poo Bah in *The Mikado* during his fourteen years with D'Oyly Carte.

The two other Edwardes shows were *My Girl,* with music by Osmond Carr, and *An Artist's Model,* with music by Sidney Jones. The Geisha was composed by Lionel Monckton and Ivan Caryll and the lyrics for all three shows were by Adrian Ross and Percy Greenbank. Ross was a prolific wordsmith, a former history professor, who penned the lyrics for scores of hit musicals including *The Merry Widow* and *Lilac Time,* in a thirty-year career. Newspaper writers were already commenting about the lavish production values. There were reports of hundreds being turned away from Edwardes shows at the Grand. The better-off patrons were urged to book in advance but the working class had to go straight from work to the theatre queue if they wanted a place in the pit or gallery.

The theatre's early success was achieved during a very competitive period. The rival Opera House had an exclusive deal with the D'Oyly Carte Opera Company and presented the Gilbert and Sullivan comic operas twice a year in the peak weeks, and a new variety theatre, the Empire, opened in 1895 and drew support with star bookings such as Marie Lloyd, Gus Elen, Charles Coborn, Bransby Williams and Cissie Loftus. The situation was partly balanced by the closure of Sergenson's rented Prince of Wales Theatre for redevelopment. He also gave up the Theatre Royal when the owners sold the property to another tenant — Yates's Wine Lodges. This was only after Sergenson had been offered the building for a bargain £16,000. He was still a town councillor and tried to interest the council in buying the site for a town hall but his colleagues snubbed the idea, even though Sergenson was not going to make a penny profit.

He must have been bitter and did not seek re-election to the council in November, 1896. The man elected in his place was W. H. Broadhead, who had been the lessee for several years of the Prince of Wales Baths, in the same block as the Prince of Wales Theatre. Broadhead went on to build a chain of theatres in the North and was Mayor of Blackpool in 1907 and 1911.

The Grand Theatre bookings for 1897 included two visits by the Kendals, which was a clear endorsement of the Grand by the brilliant and popular couple. The appeared at Easter and returned in September to premiere a comedy, *The Elder Miss Blossom,* which stayed in their repertoire for several years. A local Press reviewer welcomed them back, writing: 'Their names conjure up bright memories of happy moments listening to their homely comedy.'

Other managements were obviously keen to play the Grand and have a secure pay-day. The name of the noted producer William Greet appeared on three 1897 shows and the Shakespearean actor Edmund Tearle even accepted a January week to make his Blackpool debut in *Hamlet, Julius Caesar* and *Richard III*.

The music hall star Albert Chevalier appeared for a week in his own musical play *The Land of Nod* and he treated the Friday and Saturday audiences to interval renderings of his hit songs *Knocked 'Em in the Old Kent Road* and *My Old Dutch*. The following year another famous star of the halls, Little Tich, played weeks in June and August in a musical comedy titled *Billy*, specially written by Osmond Carr and Adrian Ross. Even on the first visit (June was a quiet month for theatres) a local reviewer declared: 'The Grand Theatre must have set another record last night, for the house was filled completely from boxes to gallery. The mighty, dramatic magnet was Little Tich, the King of laughter-makers.' Hundreds were turned away.

With regular visits of George Edwardes musicals and firm draws like the Kendals, Edward Terry, Wilson Barrett and W. S. Penley, the Grand seems to have had the advantage over the Opera House until the turn of the century, when prices for the Grand ranged from six old pence in the gallery to three shillings and sixpence ($17^1/2$p) in the stalls and grand circle. But in 1900 Sergenson had a setback when comedy actor Edward Terry, who had his own London theatre, was persuaded to transfer his annual summer week from the Grand to the Opera House by the new general manager of the Winter Gardens Company, J. R. Huddlestone, who had managed the Blackpool Empire for two years. He had quit as company secretary of the Gardens when he failed to succeed William Holland as general manager. Now Huddlestone was back and aiming to enhance his reputation.

Sergenson could afford to lose the odd show for he had an impressive programme lined up. In March the Grand was one of only four theatres to have a two-night visit by the famous Charles Wyndham and his future wife, Mary Moore, in Rostand's *Cyrano de Bergerac*. Three of George Edwardes' West End stars came to the Grand in new musical shows that all had lyrics by Adrian Ross. At Easter, Marie Studholme starred in the latest Oriental confection, *San Toy*, with music by Sidney Jones; in August Gertie Millar starred in *The Messenger Boy*, with music by Lionel Monckton (who she later married) and Ivan Caryll; and Evie Green played the lead in October in *Kitty Grey*, with music by Monckton and Howard Talbot. There were two August weeks of the American musical comedy hit *The Belle of New York*, but not with the American star Edna May, who had captivated London.

On the dramatic side, Wilson Barrett did an August week in three of his successes, *The Sign Of The Cross, The Silver King* and *The Manxman*, while the Kendals returned from another American tour to play a September week. They had a shock for Thomas Sergenson. They declined his terms for a 1901 appearance and signed with the Opera House instead.

J. R. Huddlestone scored more points over Sergenson in 1901 by booking the society actress Mrs Langtry (Lillie Langtry, the former mistress of the Prince of Wales) for her Blackpool debut in a romantic drama titled *A Royal Necklace*. To confuse matters, there was a comedienne working locally under the name 'Lily Langtry.' Some writers have assumed she was the famous Jersey Lily of royal connection but it was merely a case of the name being pinched. The real Jersey Lily always billed herself as 'Mrs Langtry' and did not sing comic songs!

Sergenson replied with the first Blackpool appearance of comedian Dan Leno in August, 1901, in producer Milton Bode's musical comedy *Orlando Dando*. The pint-sized idol of the music halls played the manager of Monsieur Toupee's hairdressing emporium. The show included speciality dances by the John Tiller Troupe.

In 1901, Thomas Sergenson's name appeared on programmes and adverts for the first time as 'Proprietor and Manager' after buying out his minor partners. He took steps to earn more from ticket sales by putting more seats in the stalls, taking space from the 'pit' area in the centre, where he could only charge a top price of one shilling (5p). The new seating plan was ready when, on the evening of January 2, 1902, the Grand was rented for a political rally at which the main speaker was the 'Young Man of Empire' and MP for Oldham, Mr Winston Churchill.

As the Opera House manager signed more star names, Sergenson replied by attracting Mrs Langtry for her next Blackpool visit and she drew large audiences for her September week in a comedy titled *Madamoiselle Mars,* by Paul Kester. She brought her own company from London's Imperial Theatre, which she was renovating at great expense. The Blackpool Gazette and News reviewer thought the playwright had also done some renovating. It was Nell Gwynne in French guise, he declared, suggesting that Paul Kester had drawn on his successful *Sweet Nell of Old Drury* to fashion a similar play about Napoleon and an actress.

Dan Leno returned to the Grand in another musical invention, *Mr Wix of Wickham,* in August. A local review said: 'He made his presence known on Monday night by drawing more people to the Grand than it has ever held before, all the newly installed seating being full for the first time.' The show was the tale of a hapless hero getting mixed up with the heirdom to the fictional Duke of Tadcaster. 'It's the way it is told that makes one laugh — and Dan Leno does the telling,' went on the reviewer. The audience was in stitches as he went through some of his music hall sketches with his inimitable patter, facial expressions and malapropisms.

Sergenson persuaded the Kendals back to the Grand for the last time in September, 1902, in *A Scrap of Paper, Still Waters Run Deep, The Elder Miss Blossom* and *Mrs Hamilton's Silence.*

A reporter gave an ecstatic welcome the same month to a new George

MEETING THE CHALLENGE

Edwardes success, *A Country Girl,* composed by Lionel Monckton with lyrics by Adrian Ross. Announcing that here was a show with an abundance of haunting tunes and an interesting story of a country girl who went to London and became a famous actress and singer, the reviewer said: 'In these days of musical comedies galore it is one of the brightest productions. The pastoral plot is quite a pleasant change to some highly-coloured contemporaries.'

Sergenson and Huddlestone continued to play one-upmanship. When the Opera House manager booked Mrs Patrick Campbell for a 1903 appearance in her most famous role, *The Second Mrs Tanqueray,* Sergenson replied with a September week by England's premier actress, Ellen Terry, in her production of Shakespeare's *Much Ado About Nothing.* She was fifty-four but still able to sweep audiences — and men — off their feet with her vivacity (four years later she married an actor twenty-three years her junior). A Gazette review said: 'Miss Terry's Beatrice is an almost perfect conception of a superb picture of womanliness, full of humour, full of sympathy and full of tender love.'

For two nights of this 1903 visit, Ellen Terry acted a programme of excerpts including the trial scene from *The Merchant of Venice,* in which she had recently played Portia, with Sir Henry Irving as Shylock, in aid of the Actor's Benevolent Fund, at Drury Lane. Her company in Blackpool included two rising stars, Matheson Lang and Harcourt Williams.

The same year Sergenson booked not one, but two Grand Theatre visits by the famous actor-manager George Alexander and his company. In the spring he appeared in the German romance *Old Heidelburg* and in the autumn he gave *If I Were King,* by Justin Huntley McCarthy. Theatre buffs may recognise this coincidence; both plays became musical comedy hits in the 1920s. The first became Sigmund Romberg's *The Student Prince* and the second became Rudolf Friml's *The Vagabond King.*

A play that had generated much notoriety was *Sappho,* adapted by the American Clyde Fitch from a scandalous novel by Alphonse Dandet. Scandalous for its time, that is. When the British actress-manager Olga Nethersole took it to New York in 1900, the police closed the show on the grounds of indecency when the heroine was carried upstairs by the hero — with obvious intentions!

In 1903 one of Miss Nethersole's companies was touring Britain in the play, with Cecile Cromwell in the main role. There was also a 'pirate' version, titled *The New Sappho,* taken from the same novel. The fates decreed that the two versions should cross paths in Blackpool, in the November. The Grand Theatre had what was advertised as the authorised version while the so-called unauthorised version, starring Annie Bell, was at the Opera House, to the great amusement of other theatre managers in the resort and the confusion of audiences.

In January, 1904, Sergenson published a list of spring and summer attractions. This may have been intended to avoid another clash of product with the Opera House. More than half the shows were advertised as being for the first time in Blackpool and included another visit by Mrs Langtry and two Wilson Barrett visits. Barrett was to play the August Bank Holiday week (which was then at the start of August) and return two weeks later. But on Saturday, July 23, ten years to the day since Barrett had opened the Grand, Sergenson received the news that Barrett had died in Liverpool.

What a useful instrument the telephone proved to be. Sergenson managed to book producer George Dance's musical comedy success, *A Chinese Honeymoon,* for August Bank Holiday, and Miss Fortescue in *The School For Scandal* later in August.

The September visit of Mrs Langtry was billed by Sergenson as 'a stupendous attraction.' The actress had just returned from one of her famous American tours in her new success, a comedy titled *Mrs Dering's Divorce,* by Percy Fendall. She started her new British tour at the Grand but a local newspaper review was less than enthusiastic. The reporter thought the play a little hackneyed. The story-line had perhaps been driven round the block too often. But it drew the usual large audiences for the Jersey Lily's visits and was well received. The play gave the principals plenty of scope to demonstrate their abilities, said the writer. This was probably a polite way of saying, in journalistic parlance, that it was a very suitable device for Mrs Langtry to parade round the stage in her fine gowns by Worth, of Paris.

Competition at this stage of Blackpool's entertainment life had become intense. As well as the rejuvenated Opera House under J. R. Huddlestone's management, there was the Tower Company's new Palace Variety Theatre, which had emerged from the bankrupt Alhambra development on the Promenade, and renewed opposition from the Hippodrome (formerly the Empire) after two or three troubled years. There was all day entertainment in the Tower and Winter Gardens buildings and pierrot shows had become popular on the Central and South piers.

The astute Sergenson, an independent operator in an arena now occupied by well-funded public companies, showed no sign of buckling. He even set the pace by staging a couple of 'flying matinees' in the spring of 1905. These became a popular practice, with theatre managements bringing in special 'one-off' afternoon shows by artistes who were appearing for the week in inland towns. Mrs Langty gave one March matinee in the play *Mrs Dering's Divorce,* while comedian George Robey with a 'select concert company' played another.

Then he came up with another typical coup — one of the greatest of his career — in presenting the great French actress, Sarah Bernhardt, and Mrs Patrick Campbell, in a single matinee performance of Maeterlinck's *Pelleas and Melisande,* on Wednesday, July 19, 1905. Sergenson had a packed house, mostly ladies, and all records must have been broken, wrote a reporter. He also mentioned Mdme Bernhardt's first Blackpool appearance in 1882, saying history must deal kindly with it, for her second visit was a great personal triumph.

'The name of the sixty-year-old tragedienne is as magnetic as her personality. It was the person that drew, not the play. The name of the so-called Belgian

MEETING THE CHALLENGE

Shakespeare, Maurice Maeterlinck, is but known to the cult. The general public know him not; and certainly had they known the nature of Pelleas et Melisande, we doubt if there would have been half the house there was', he declared. It was performed in French. There followed a brief review praising the cast and a long explanation of the plot of this romantic tragedy.

Musical shows from George Edwardes and other producers continued to be the Grand's money-spinners although the romantic musical comedy was losing its appeal in London. A review of *The Orchid*, another composition of Lionel Monckton and Ivan Caryll, said: 'It seems ages since we had one of Mr George Edwardes' combinations of pretty girls with delightful dresses, dainty dances and charming songs. However, Blackpool is being treated to the very latest and greatest of the musical play successes and, perhaps, the last for a while, for we are told they are no longer in fashion. Blackpool and its visitors evidently do not agree for the Grand Theatre was pleasantly crowded on Monday night . . .'

This type of show did, in fact, remain very popular in the provinces and touring versions made good profits for London producers who were making little money in the West End. *The Orchid*, and two other musical successes of that year, *The Cingalee* and *The Duchess of Dantzig,* each made two visits to the Grand. Profits also rolled in for Thomas Sergenson from the newest Marie Studholme show, *Lady Madcap,* the ever-popular *Charley's Aunt*, and a week's visit after a lapse of many years by Edward Compton's Comedy Company, in the old English comedies *The School for Scandal, The Reformed Rake, She Stoops to Conquer* and *Davy Garrick.*

The shows mentioned above enabled Sergenson to weather a storm of competition, in 1905, from the expensive, big star programmes put on by other local theatres. For instance, the Hippodrome's strong line-up included a week's visit by the famous American escapologist Harry Houdini; the Palace Varieties had a consistently high standard with headliners like Vesta Tilley and Nellie Wallace; while J.R. Huddlestone's star concerts at the Winter Gardens included international musical names like the American 'march king' John Philip Sousa, the operatic prima donna Melba, and the violin virtuoso Fritz Kreisler.

In 1906, the Grand's proprietor strengthened his position in the field of drama with actors like Beerbohm Tree and Frank Benson. And Sergenson became the first manager to present an Ibsen play in Blackpool.

There was praise in February from a Gazette and News reviewer, who wrote: 'Not often does Blackpool have the opportunity of seeing the genius of Shakespeare played by a company of the calibre of that toured by Mr F.R. Benson, the great exponent of the immortal Bard. Mr Sergenson ought to be rewarded for his enterprise by crowded houses every evening.'

In May there were more kind words from the cultured Gazette reviewer when the Grand presented H.V. Neilson's touring company in Ibsen's *A Doll's House*. No-one should miss this first chance to see an Ibsen play, he wrote. It had been the subject of a great amount of discussion and some had ventured

Wilson Barrett and Maud Jeffries in Barrett's own play,
'The Sign Of The Cross.'

W.S. Penley made 'Charley's Aunt' famous and often played it at the Grand.

Ellen Terry came to the Grand in 1903 in her production of 'As You Like It.'

Lillie Langtry, who billed herself Mrs Langtry, starred at the Grand three times.

to suggest the play was immoral, the reviewer pointed out. But an observing mind would not make that mistake.

'The theme is really the emancipation of women and the problem is put before us with such psychological power as to make this one of the great dramas of the day. No wonder, therefore, that it has been played in nearly every language in Europe, as well as all over North America.'

One wonders how Blackpool society, in 1906, reacted to the reviewer's explanation that Ibsen had used the character of Nora Helmer as the medium 'through which the spirit of Woman is seen struggling through the ages against darkness, ignorance and serfdom.' And her husband Torvald 'stands for all that is conventional in Man: the embodiment of centuries of custom and tradition, and therefore out of sympathy with the demands of Woman to be his equal.'

The further explanation that Nora's struggle to break away from the slavery was not a loosening of the marriage tie, probably did little to quell the outrage of the men who bothered to read the review.

The Opera House continued to present the popular Mr and Mrs Kendal. In 1906 they appeared for a week in September, but the Grand's owner eclipsed them with one of his big name coups. He presented a three-day programme starring Beerbohm Tree, Britain's leading actor since the death the previous year of Sir Henry Irving.

There were more words of approval in the Gazette. 'Much is termed acting when it is but a pleasing elocutionary display,' whereas Mr Tree was a real artist, explained the reviewer. The great actor could change his voice, appearance and movement to become the character. Tree brought his company, including Constance Collier, in three plays: Sidney Grundy's *Business Is Business*, Kipling's *The Man Who Never Was* and Thackeray's *Colonel Newcombe*.

The Ibsen week must have been successful because Sergenson put on another of the Norwegian playwright's dramas the following spring. He engaged Leigh Lovel and Octavia Kenmore's touring company in *The Master Builder* and the couple came back in 1908 with three — *Hedda Gabler, A Doll's House* and *The Master Builder.*

There was also new blood on the musical side. Producer Robert Courtneidge, after a couple of co-productions with George Edwardes, had his own West End hit in *The Blue Moon*, which he sent to the Grand for a week in September, 1906. The star was Florence Smithson and it was described in the local Press as 'Operatic musical comedy of the highest order.' The co-writer of the story was a former Blackpool man, A.M. Thompson, who was well known under the journalistic name of 'Dangle'. The music was by Ivan Caryll and Paul Rubens. Another Courtneidge success, which he co-wrote with A.M. Thompson, was *The Dairymaids*, which played at the Grand for the August Bank Holiday week in 1907 and introduced to Blackpool the beautiful, sixteen-year-old darling of the London stage, Phyllis Dare.

A reviewer in the Gazette and News thought she was 'a darling little lady' who would sing and dance her way into the hearts of local playgoers. The show launched a sparkling career and a million picture postcards of Phyllis Dare, whose sister Zena was at the Opera House the same week with Seymour Hicks in a comedy titled *Papa's Wife*. The sisters did not actually star together in any show until 1940, when they were in an Ivor Novello comedy at the Grand Theatre.

The greatest event at the Grand in 1908 — and every other theatre that was lucky enough to book the show — was the first visit of *The Merry Widow*. This Viennese musical by Franz Lehar was brought to London by George Edwardes and opened at Daly's Theatre in June, 1907, two years after its initial success in Vienna. It caused a sensation all over the world and became the most popular musical comedy ever. It has been noted that on one particular evening in its early years, it was being performed in four hundred towns and cities. In most Continental productions the title role of Sonia was played by ladies of operatic girth. George Edwardes, famous for romantic shows in which the leading ladies were always slim and glamorous, had the show radically improved for the English stage and made the merry widow slim and beautiful in the figure of twenty-one-year-old Lily Elsie, who had previously played only secondary roles. She became a star overnight. Five other actresses who played Sonia in London or on tour were all under thirty. In the show's first Blackpool visit in April, 1908, the role was played by Gertrude Lester and Danilo was played by Basil S. Foster.

For weeks before the show came to the Grand, the box office had a constant stream of inquiries. Sergenson took the unusual step of placing newspaper ads which merely stated the date on which tickets would go on sale. They were soon sold. Hundreds were turned away from every peformance. Mr and Mrs Kendal, making their usual Easter week visit to the Opera House, were put in the shade.

A local reviewer, noting that the musical had been a goldmine for music publishers and theatre managements, wrote: 'It is hard to explain why so many of the musical plays presented to us have attained such popularity but the question, put in regard to *The Merry Widow*, is easily answered. No English production of the kind has its wealth of music, its delightful songs and choruses and, above all, so captivating a waltz. When *The Merry Widow* is but a memory in Blackpool the piece will be recalled first of all for the waltz and next for the song *Vilia,* with its longing, fascinating chorus.' There was no mention for Adrian Ross, the man whose English lyrics contributed so much to the show's success. Lyric writers, then and now, tend to be taken for granted. *The Merry Widow* was rebooked for an August week and returned frequently to the Grand for five years and was revived four times in the next fifty years.

There were other major successes at the Grand in the summer of 1908. The handsome Seymour Hicks appeared in his own play *The Gay Gordons* with Zena Dare, in August, and a month later Hicks brought the show back for a week with his wife, Ellaline Terriss, in her original role. Robert Courtneidge provided another visit of Phyllis Dare in *The Dairymaids* and Courtneidge presented his new comic opera success, *Tom Jones,* written in collaboration with A.M. Thompson, from Henry Fielding's novel of the same name. The stars of the Blackpool visit were Harry Welchman, in his first leading role, Ruth Vincent, Carrie Moore and comedian Dan Rolyat. Autumn attractions included George Alexander and Irene Vanbrugh in *The Thief*, by Cosmo Hamilton; Marie Studholme in a musical comedy, *My Mimosa Maid*, and the society actress Mrs Brown Potter in Somerset Maugham's *Lady Frederick*.

The year 1908 was significant for the Grand in that Thomas Sergenson finally acknowledged the threat of the new motion picture houses and he bought the latest Bioscope projection equipment which he introduced in March under the name Grando Bioscope. The system was used only occasionally in 1908 but formed an important part of Sergenson's programming in 1909, a vital year for the owner-manager.

CHAPTER FIVE

Sergenson's Ploy

If Thomas Sergenson has impressed as a competent manager and showman, then his final year of ownership of the Grand Theatre was very much in character. During his 1908 season of expensive, and presumably successful, attractions, there was growing competition from the town's two cinemas, the Colosseum and the Hippodrome. There was talk of plans for the first purpose-built cinema, the Royal Pavilion. A wise man would have seen changing tastes and new commercial pressures ahead. Sergenson could also have been concerned about the need for refurbishment and alterations, for the Grand had been open fourteen years.

He apparently decided that the days of the owner-manager were numbered and he let it be known that he was open to offers for the Grand. If there were any offers, they were not acceptable.

Sergenson decided to ensure some revenue from the unpredictable winter months by leasing the Grand for three months to T. Allan Edwardes, who owned variety theatres in Derby, Sheffield and Stoke-on-Trent. This could even have been a 'trial run' with a view to purchase. At the start of November, 1908, Edwardes introduced what he advertised as 'the best value entertainment in Blackpool' with prices from only two old pence to one shilling and sixpence ($7^1/2$p). These were on a par with cinema prices. Edwardes also introduced twice-nightly shows to Blackpool, forcing the rival Palace (owned by the Tower Company) to follow suit.

There were few well known variety names on the programmes but Edwardes shocked the town's other managers with one superstar week in December. It was the first variety tour of the operatic prima donna Emma Albani, who had occasionally done Sunday concerts at the Winter Gardens at fancy prices. A reviewer wrote that the peerless queen of song, in her first appearance on the vaudeville stage, had a great reception from crowded houses. She sang operatic arias and some popular songs and said of the Grand Theatre: 'What a fine hall it is to sing in.'

After the three-month rental, no buyer materialised for the Grand. Sergenson resumed his management on February 1, 1909. Looking at his truly bizarre mixture of bookings for the year, it is reasonable to assume that he set out to build a bumper balance sheet and pull audiences from the Palace Varieties. From February to Easter he ran five weeks of cheap and cheery variety, two weeks of pantomime, two plays and one musical comedy. The variety weeks included obvious economy measures like talent contests and wrestling challenges.

For the Easter weeks, when big money could be made from good shows, Sergenson secured two brilliant new shows from the George Edwardes organisation. Both were by contemporary Viennese composers who were meeting a popular demand created by the success of *The Merry Widow*. The first show to arrive, prior to its London opening, was *A Dollar Princess,* set in California and featuring a headstrong girl in a tale that appeared to have been borrowed from Shakespeare's *The Taming of the Shrew*. The composer was Leo Fall and a review said the show had an abundance of haunting songs and waltzes. The stars were Robert Michaelis, Alice Pollard, Hilda Moody and Kitty Gordon.

The second show was *A Waltz Dream*, a romantic operetta about princesses and handsome hussars. A local reviewer said it was 'a bright, pretty example of the new musical comedy of the Viennese type'. It was appearing for the first time out of London with a strong West End company including Robert Evett, Amy Augarde and May De Souza. The lush, romantic score was by Oscar Straus (not one of the famous Strauss family) and, like *The Merry Widow*, both these new Viennese shows had been adapted from the German and livened up for the English stage by librettist Basil Hood. The English lyrics were again by Adrian Ross.

Between Easter and the Whitsuntide holiday, Sergenson offered a strong list of plays, mainly comedies such as Somerset Maugham's *Mrs Dot* and Frederick Lonsdale's *The Early Worm*. For the busy Whit holiday week it was back to higher ticket prices with *The Merry Widow*, which was placarded

Some of the big shows presented by Thomas Sergenson in his last year of ownership of the Grand Theatre.

as 'the play that is still breaking records all over the world.'

June has never been a wonderful month for seaside theatres, falling between seasons. Sergenson appears to have decided not to take any risks with plays and opted for variety shows supported by Bioscope short films. It probably hurt the box office at the nearby Palace Varieties. July brought a programme of contemporary plays and the onset of the main holiday season resulted in a switch to big name shows that could play to high capacity at enhanced prices.

The August Bank Holiday week attraction was Marie Studholme in the musical play *Miss Hook of Holland*, by Paul Rubens, and then came the first provincial showing of *The King of Cadonia*, a recent musical success. The demand for more Viennese melodies was met by return visits of *The Merry Widow* and *A Waltz Dream*. This glossy 1909 season should have included the latest London success, Lionel Monckton's *The Arcadians*, which had been advertised at the Grand as a forthcoming attraction. There must have been a hitch because producer Robert Courtneidge held the show back. A famous visitor to the Grand on August 28 was the Italian tenor Enrico Caruso, who watched part of the musical show *Havana*, starring Dorothy Ward, from the rear of the stalls. Caruso was in the resort for a concert at the Winter Gardens the following evening.

Ellaline Terriss starred in the musical play *The Dashing Little Duke*, by her husband, Seymour Hicks, but with the summer season fading the accent went back to plays. They included Alfred Sutro's *The Walls of Jericho*, starring the former D'Oyly Carte principal, Rutland Barrington. Before each show

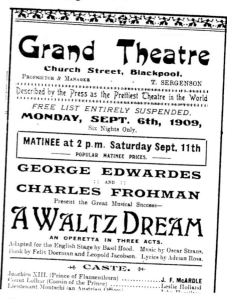

he treated the audience to what was billed as his 'inimitable entertainment at the piano.'

The old Sergenson showmanship burst forth in the week of October 18, when the Blackpool Flying Week was held at Squires Gate. The British Bioscope Company sent a team to town to film the magnificent men in their rickety flying machines in Britain's first major flying display. The films were processed overnight and shown every afternoon at Sergenson's special flying week matinees at the Grand, ruining the variety matinees at the Palace. The daily film shows made everyone aware that moving pictures were passing the stage of being gimmicks and were becoming an attraction in their own right.

Working on the experience of T. Allen Edwardes the previous winter, Sergenson booked his own variety season to start on November 1. He placed the emphasis on novelty, with the headline acts being illusionists, pugilists and weightlifters. Sergenson engaged Alfred Selwyn of the Collins Music Hall, London, as director of varieties, and went on holiday. On his return there was a call from George Harrop, the general manager of the mighty Blackpool Tower Company. The Tower management could have been fed up with Sergenson's aggressive policy of scheduling variety shows in the off-season periods, to the detriment of receipts at the Palace Varieties. They would have also been aware that the Grand Theatre could make a lot of money in the summer. Negotiations for the purchase of the Grand must have been going on when the theatre closed on Saturday, December 11, 'for annual cleaning'.

The surprise news of the sale to the Tower Company was given in the Christmas Eve edition of the Gazette and News. The report said that negotiations had been conducted in great secrecy and the price would not be known until Tower Company shareholders had been notified. But the newspaper doubted that the company would pay as much as £45,000, which Sergenson had been asking earlier in the year.

So there was a further surprise in the New Year when the price was revealed — a handsome £47,500, leaving Sergenson with £31,000 after clearance of the mortgage and other liabilities. The local business pundits had under-estimated Sergenson. Only a strong balance sheet, coupled with Sergenson's ploy in competing with the Palace Varieties, would have persuaded the prudent Tower Company to part with so much money.

For Thomas Sergenson it was a fitting finale to a long career as the resort's most consistently successful showman. His achievements surely put him ahead of William Holland, general manager of the Winter Gardens Company from 1887 to his death in 1895, yet Holland has always been given more attention in print.

Sergenson, as a one-man operator in a precarious business, had competed with the Winter Gardens Company for twenty-nine years and had prospered in spite of their best efforts with the Opera House. Finally, he had had the audacity to turn his sights on the mighty Tower Company and had retired with the proceeds!

Report in the Gazette-News, December 24, 1909

It has been remarked during the last few days that there seemed to be nothing stirring in Blackpool but yesterday information was officially communicated that will provide something of a sensation to be talked about during the Christmas holidays. Today the Grand Theatre, with the suite of offices and shops alongside in Church Street, and the two shops and offices adjacent to Her Majesty's Opera House further up the street, are in the hands of the Blackpool Tower Company and under the management of Mr George H. Harrop. Such news was quite unexpected for the fact that negotiations for purchase by the Tower Company had been under way for some time had been kept profoundly secret.

Yesterday afternoon, the Chairman of the Tower Company, Alderman J. Bickerstaffe, who was accompanied by the secretary, Mr Robert Parker, gave a short address in the directors' board room to an audience consisting only of gentlemen of the Press.

Brevity is the soul of business! The speech consisted of but one sentence: 'The Blackpool Tower and Palace Company have purchased the Grand Theatre with the shops adjoining and also the shops adjacent to the Opera House.' That was all. To questions about the price the chairman smiled and the secretary became Sphinx-like. The shareholders would be told first.

It may be interesting to know that the price which Mr Sergenson was asking some time ago was about £45,000 but we think our readers may take it for granted that the sum paid by the Tower Company will not be so large. All the chairman would say about the price was 'We are satisfied' — and he looked it!

The chairman said that they had taken over Mr Sergenson's engagements for the Christmas and New Year weeks, then would close until Easter — 'for we intend to spend a lot of money on renovations, alterations and so on.'

(Two weeks later, the Gazette carried a report that was much more informative. The paper reported that a Tower Company circular to shareholders stated the price paid for the Grand and the other properties was £47,500. So much for the paper's earlier theory that the Tower Company would knock the price down!)

The circular told the shareholders: "It is freehold and free from chief rent and is situated on the main business thoroughfare of Blackpool. The property is modern, well constructed and in every way admirably adapted for business purposes. The theatre has full dramatic and music, singing and stage dancing licences and licensed refreshment bars. Accommodation for 3,000 people can be given in the theatre, which was designed by the eminent architect Mr Frank Matcham. It is recognised, in its perfect architectural features, as 'Matcham's masterpiece'. The purchase price for the whole of the property . . . is the sum of £31,020, subject to an existing mortgage on the Grand Theatre and adjacent shops of £16,480, carrying interest at the rate of £4 per centum per annum, thus making a total purchase price of £47,500. The shops and offices are well tenanted and produce a total average yearly rent of £1,000."

Just before the reopening of the Grand, the Gazette News published the following report on March 18, 1910:

The Grand Theatre, Blackpool, which will be reopened on Monday, has undergone a wonderful transformation since it came under the control of the Tower Company a few months ago. From floor to ceiling it has been completely overhauled, repainted, redecorated, reupholstered and, in one or two of its features, remodernised and reconstructed. Previously the theatre was described as one of the prettiest of its size in the world today; its right to the title will be difficult to dispute.

The decoration, upholstering and draping have been carried out to such a very elaborate scale that whether viewed from the highest seat in the gallery or from any part in the auditorium, the theatre presents a picture of splendour and luxury. Those familiar with the work of F. de Jong and Company, the noted theatre decorators, who were responsible for the artistic adornment of the Tower and Palace ballrooms, and the Tower Circus, will find that the decoration of the Grand is one of the choicest examples of their work.

The general colour scheme is lighter and more attractive than formerly, the prevailing tones being cream, rose du barri, varying shades of crimson and rich old gold. The ceiling has been most artistically treated, the existing adornments having been elaborately and greatly improved, while above the proscenium are two panels representing music and mirth, beautifully painted in oils by Mr J. Loss, one of de Jong's chief artists. The face of the grand circle is also rich in ornamentation, hand painted floral panels on a background of gold being strikingly pretty.

The low corridors and staircases are bright with white enamel and the walls are covered with an artistic Japanese paper with raised gold figuring on a cream background. The walls of the pit and upper circle have been decorated with a crimson flock of a neat design and in the gallery terracotta and a crimson dado blend harmoniously. The grand circle saloon bar has been decorated throughout in pure white and gold, with panels of white French anaglypta while that of the upper circle has been treated with crimson ingrained paper, and the ceiling painted with a design characteristic of the Adam style.

A great improvement has been affected by altering the rake of the floor, which has been entirely relaid. The stall accommodation has been increased from 100 to 300 seats, and at the back of the pit, to avoid draughts, a revolving shutter has been introduced. The stage has been entirely refloored.

The doorway leading to the stalls, being reconstructed, gives more comfortable access and other improvements will be noted.

Bickerstaffe and Company have done all the draping, upholstering and carpeting under the supervision of the firm's general manager, Mr F. Hornblow. The scheme is carried out in a pleasing electric blue Utrecht velvet, the carpets of rich, super Wilton being in keeping. The seats in the pit and upper circle are now all covered with this velvet and the gallery seats with a queer sort of leathery fabric. Electric lighting has been practically renewed.

CHAPTER SIX
The New Regime

THE Tower Company wasted no time in refurbishing the Grand. As soon as the festive season attraction had moved out, the new owners closed the theatre for an elaborate and expensive face-lift. The work took ten weeks and just before the reopening a feature article in the Gazette and News described the improvements. From floor to ceiling the Grand Theatre had been overhauled, painted, decorated, upholstered, carpeted and structurally changed, said the article. Everything had been done in an ornate manner and the theatre presented a picture of splendour and luxury.

The general colour scheme in the auditorium was lighter, the main tones being cream and rose du barri, with backgrounds of crimson and old gold. The job had been undertaken by the specialist theatre decorators, F. de Jong and Company. The ceiling of the Grand, said the article, 'has been treated most artistically, the existing adornments having been elaborately and greatly improved, while above the proscenium are two panels representing music and mirth, painted beautifully in oils by Mr J. Loss, one of de Jong's chief artists.' The seats, carpets and drapes had been fitted by the Blackpool firm of Bickerstaffe and Company, the seats in an electric blue Utrecht velvet. The stage had been refloored, a new safety curtain fitted, and the electric lighting and wiring renewed, the article went on.

There had been several structural changes. The doorway to the stalls had been enlarged to give easier access and the floor of the stalls had been relaid to give a better rake. The stalls seating capacity had been increased from one to three hundred by eliminating the low-priced pit area. The reference in the article to the new stalls flooring clears up the puzzlement in a consultant's report in 1977, when the Grand was refurbished after five years of closure. The consultant wondered what had happened to the lovely hardwood floor described in Press articles on the opening of the Grand in 1894.

The theatre reopened on Monday, March 21, 1910, under the management of Percy Harrop, the son of the Tower Company's general manager, George W. Harrop. It was the week before Easter and the attraction was the musical *The Dollar Princess,* the same show as presented by Thomas Sergenson the previous Easter. A strong cast was headed by Leonard Mackay, Eric Thorne, W. Louis Bradfield, Daisy Elliston and Clara Evelyn. But the Winter Gardens Company had taken steps to blunt the grand reopening with a coup at their rival Opera House. They had secured the huge London success, producer Robert Courtneidge's *The Arcadians,* which Thomas Sergenson had provisionally booked for the Grand the previous summer, only to be disappointed.

The Tower Company were now in the 'legitimate' theatre business and had a successful first season, although not as star-studded as 1909's. The company managed to book *The Arcadians* for a week in August with the same cast, headed by Walter Passmore and Veronica Brady. This legendary musical show had been a gamble for Robert Courtneidge. It was set in the fantasy kingdom of Arcadia — and such theatrical flights of fancy were not favoured by conservative-minded investors. Courtneidge sank his own money into the show and it was still running at his London theatre, the Shaftesbury, with Alfred Lester, Phyllis Dare, Harry Welchman and Dan Rolyat among the principals. Among the lesser ranks was the producer's daughter, sixteen-year-old Cicely Courtneidge, who was soon to take over, Phyllis Dare's role.

Former Blackpool man A.M. Thompson had written the show in collaboration with Mark Ambient and the music was by Lionel Monckton and Howard Talbot. Monckton was in his most prolific period — for he had also composed the Gaiety Theatre success *Our Miss Gibbs,* the romantic tale of a Harrods sales girl. The touring version twice played the Grand in 1910 with Alice Pollard, George Gregory and Lionel Mackinder in the leading roles. Yet another Lionel Monckton hit, *The Quaker Girl,* had opened in London.

On the dramatic side in 1910, the Grand had the provincial premiere, in July, of *The Speckled Band,* a Sherlock Holmes mystery by Arthur Conan Doyle, while in September the theatre figured early in the tour of *Dr Jekyll and Mr Hyde,* which starred H.B. Irving, the elder son of Sir Henry Irving.

The Tower Company closed the Grand on November 5, the earliest winter closure until then. The Opera House also announced a six month closure for extensive rebuilding and transferred its engagements to the Winter Gardens Pavilion. The rebuilding project, obviously made necessary by the Grand's new opulence and comfort, gave the Opera House a larger seating capacity than the Grand. Faced with this, the Tower Company used the winter to make even more improvements at the Grand, mainly to the stage lighting and the upper circle seating. They certainly could not squeeze any more seating accommodation into the compact theatre.

The policy of a long winter closure was to last until 1917. The Tower Company had a venue that could clear £500 a week in summer; quite a tidy sum in those days. But November has always brought a chill to theatre receipts in the resort. Without the holiday crowds Blackpool becomes a small town on a windy, rainswept coast where theatre-going can require a bit of bravery. This was the case even when entertainment was not available at the flick of a switch by a warm fireside. The Tower Company management were quite content to let their Palace variety theatre cater for the locals in winter, leaving the Opera House to look after the town's cultural needs!

Thomas Sergenson had done well to get out of the business with a handsome profit because popular entertainment was on the verge of radical change. From across the Atlantic came the anarchic sounds of a new music called ragtime. It gave the shivers to theatre owners and producers who had grown fat on operetta and musical comedy. The strident new sound was said to have dismayed George Edwardes, whose melodic touring shows had contributed much to the success of the Grand Theatre. Ragtime had a world-wide boost in 1911 with Irving Berlin's hit, *Alexander's Ragtime Band,* and the composer himself came to London in 1912, sending shockwaves through the world of sedate music.

Theatre owners faced a new form of show called revue. This, too, seemed anarchic. They said it just unravelled in a string of unrelated songs, dances and sketches. And there was a third threat. It came from the rapid development of motion pictures. They were pulling more patrons from the live theatre and would eventually overwhelm it.

By operating a summer seasonal policy, the Grand Theatre was able to carry on as if nothing new was happening. The resort's population more than doubled in the season, providing what amounted to a big city audience for shows. Then there was 'the Blackpool factor.' Visitors were conservative in their tastes. They were happy with familiar forms of entertainment. They liked to know what they were spending their hard-earned brass on.

This was good news for melodic musicals. In 1911 producer George Edwardes sent Lionel Monckton's new hit, *The Quaker Girl,* to the Grand for Easter, eclipsing Monckton's *The Arcadians,* which was at the Opera House. *The Quaker Girl,* later regarded by some cirtics as Monckton's finest show, starred Leonard Mackay and Alice Pollard, and it returned for an even busier week in August.

The Merry Widow, in its fourth year of touring, was still considered strong enough to be the Grand's Whit Week bill and in August there was an ambitious Edwardes week of his three Viennese productions, *The Merry Widow, A Waltz Dream* and *The Dollar Princess,* each show playing two nights. No producer would attempt such a feat today! Disaster struck at the weekend when a national rail strike left all the scenery and effects stranded in Blackpool.

Lyric writer Adrian Ross had penned the songs in *The Quaker Girl* and also for another new Edwardes show at the Grand in 1911, *The Girl In The Train.* This was another Viennese musical of librettist Victor Leon (who co-wrote *The Merry Widow)* and the music was by Leo Fall, composer of *The Dollar Princess.* One of the principals of *The Girl In The Train* was Lauri de Frece, the younger brother of Walter de Frece, the variety agent and husband of Vesta Tilley. In the Twenties, as Sir Walter de Frece, he was the MP for Blackpool. Lauri de Frece was a leading light comedy artist who often appeared at the Grand. In 1914 he married Fay Compton but they separated before Lauri's early death from peritonitis in 1921.

In September, 1911, two plays were presented at the Grand by Laurence Irving, the younger son of Sir Henry Irving. Laurence appeared with his wife, Mabel Hackney, in his own play, *The Unwritten Law,* and in *The Lily,* by the American dramatist-producer David Belasco. (The actor and his wife died when the Empress of Ireland sank after a collision in the St Lawrence River, Canada, in 1914).

The week after the Irvings' Blackpool visit, a great future star worked backstage at the Grand on a touring production of *The Blue Bird,* a fantasy play by Maurice

Maeterlinck. The future star was Claude Rains, who was stage manager for Frederick Harrison's touring company. He played his first stage roles when the company visited Australia later in the year.

Apart from three festive weeks of pantomimes, the Grand was closed by the owners from November 4 to March 25, 1912, opening with the big Easter attraction of *The Count of Luxembourg,* second of three Franz Lehar shows produced in Britain by George Edwardes. The lyrics, almost inevitably, were by Adrian Ross.

After the show's London premiere, in May, 1911, the critics were in raptures. 'Never has there been such a bright, merry and unflagging musical comedy,' wrote one. 'Franz Lehar's music is so clever and resourceful that it should be held up as a pattern for other musical comedies.'

It is interesting to note the reference to musical comedy. Today we look upon the Viennese musicals as operettas and they are occasionally revived by major opera companies as the lighter side of a repertoire. The critic's comment about *The Count of Luxembourg* being a model for other shows was his observation on the mediocrity of some musical comedies of the era. The stars of the show's 1912 visit were Robert Michaelis, Phyllis Le Grand, Eric Thorne and Lauri de Frece.

In June, 1912, after the 'enormous attraction' of Harold Neville and his company in Shakespeare's *Twelfth Night,* the Tower Company introduced a new policy to tackle the well known flat spots in Blackpool's theatregoing habits. June had always been a quiet month so the company arranged for producer J.M. Brown to stage a short repertory season of contemporary plays. The idea was often used by the Tower Company at the Grand, right through to the Sixties.

There was a spate of eastern spectaculars just before World War One, led by Edward Knoblock's *Kismet.* The touring version produced by George Dance was booked for three weeks in August 1912 — the longest in the theatre's history to that date. This story of desert hatred, bloodshed, love and revenge had dazzling, enormous sets — a harem, a bath, a mosque — with camels and other livestock to add atmosphere to outdoor scenes.

The two Easter attractions in 1913 were duly provided by George Edwardes. A new Franz Lehar success, *Gipsy Love,* with English lyrics by Adrian Ross, starred Leonard Mackay and Lauri de Frece, and a Paul Rubens musical comedy, *The Sunshine Girl,* starred Phyllis Dare in her original Gaiety Theatre role. The important Whit holiday period was also filled by yet another Lionel Monckton show, *The Dancing Mistress,* produced by George Edwardes, and four prime weeks of August and September were occupied by Edwardes productions, including what was advertised as a farewell tour of *The Merry Widow.*

There was another strong week in September when the famous actor-manager George Alexander, who had recently been knighted, appeared with his St James's Theatre Company in *Bella Donna,* by J.B. Fagan, the story of a female poisoner. Mrs Patrick Campbell had appeared opposite Sir George in the London production but she was not on the tour.

THE NEW REGIME

Before the First World War the Theatre Royal, Drury Lane, was noted for a series of spectacular dramas. One was a racing thriller titled *The Whip,* which producer George Dance toured in 1914, visiting the Grand in August, just after war was declared. In a sensational closing scene depicting the Two Thousand Guineas classic, three racehorses were seen at full gallop on a revolving track fixed to the stage.

The horses were got into their stride before the curtains went back to show them going at full tilt against a moving backcloth of a racecourse. On the opening night the horse nearest the audience strumbled and fell, its hooves just missing the drummer in the orchestra pit. A strong tethering rein prevented the horse falling into the pit. Such was the ambitious style of stage productions in those days, when producers strived for visual impact — and larger audiences.

The musical offering of 1914 and 1915 failed to keep up the momentum of preceeding years. The Edwardes organisation was in decline and the famous producer's death revealed a financial problem that led to his company falling back on just one London theatre, Daly's.

The Edwardes company's lease on London's Gaiety Theatre was taken over by the light comedy actor George Grossmith Jnr, a former Edwardes star and son of a great Savoyard and humourist of the late nineteenth century. The first big success of the younger Grossmith and his partner, Edward Laurillard, was *Tonight's The Night,* a musical play set against the background of a masked ball at Covent Garden.

It was the first hit of author and librettist Fred Thompson, an architectural student who had switched his talents to the theatre. The show had toured the United States in 1914 and when it returned to London it had acquired some Jerome Kern songs, including *They Didn't Believe Me.* A tour of the show visited the Grand in August, 1915, and on two later visits the cast included Jack Buchanan, forging a career that would make him a West End, Broadway and Hollywood star for thirty-five years.

For two weeks in April, 1915, the pioneer of the repertory system, Miss Horniman, from Manchester's Gaiety Theatre, brought her company to the Grand for the first time, presenting John Galsworthy's *The Fugutive* and in October the theatre was the venue for the first Blackpool performance of Bernard Shaw's *Pygmalion,* a London success for Beerbohm Tree and Mrs Patrick Campbell (who was forty-nine when she played Eliza Doolittle). Blackpool saw Charles Macdona's touring company in the play.

The Grand closed for the winter earlier than ever — on October 31 — and apart from three festive season weeks it was closed until mid-March, 1916, as the management again followed a policy of caution.

It opened with a show that was advertised as the 'enormous attraction' of American star Raymond Hitchcock in a musical farce by Fred Thompson, titled *Mr Manhattan.* Produced by Grossmith and Laurillard, this was the first major show to be both rehearsed and premiered at the Grand Theatre. George Grossmith was there to supervise matters.

The plot was typical of farce. Man about town, out of town for a while, had a wily butler who rented out the apartment for a few days. Then all sorts of people turned up unexpectedly — including the master! In the cast, as an ageing playboy, was Austin Melford, the call-boy during the Grand's opening week in 1894.

Local theatregoers were becoming better informed through the introduction of a new type of newspaper feature, the show business column. It appeared in the Friday issue of the thrice-weekly Gazette and Herald under the title of Stage Whispers, by E.J. Dromgoole.

In praising *Mr Manhattan* at the Grand, Dromgoole wrote: 'There is quite a noble difference between a musical play and a revue. In the play the ladies are generally well dressed; in a revue they are invariably half dressed. This is a play!' Mr Dromgoole thus stated his philosophy and would repeatedly speak out against what he thought was poor taste on the stage.

One of the more popular thrillers of the time was a Chinese piece called *Mr Wu,* by H.M. Vernon and Harold Owen, which had helped make Matheson Lang's name with a year's run at the Strand Theatre. Lang brought the play to the Grand in July, 1916, and a reviewer said he gave an absorbing, convincing study as the curious character of the title. It was set in Hong Kong and had 'thrilling situations, cleverly worked out story and fine characterisations.'

In 1916 composer Paul Rubens' name was on three shows sent on tour by the Edwardes organisation from Daly's Theatre. *The Miller's Daughters* and *Tina* each made two visits to the Grand. The third, *The Happy Days,* was his final work. For years Rubens had courted the lovely Phyllis Dare and they eventually became engaged. But their story was far from happy. Rubens discovered he had a terminal illness and broke the engagement. He died in 1917, aged forty-one. Phyllis Dare, the star of the London production of *The Happy Days,* never married.

Like most musical comedy composers of the period, Rubens came from a well-to-do background and studied law at Oxford. For twenty years he wrote 'name' shows for George Edwardes and other producers and was one of the few composers to write his own lyrics.

Adrian Ross followed the same path into the theatre after a history degree at Oxford. His lyrics graced sixteen shows that had West End runs of more than five hundred performances; probably a record.

Lionel Monckton, the best remembered musical comedy composer of the era, came from a wealthy family and was the music critic of the Daily Telegraph. He married Gertie Millar, whose brilliance earned her the title 'Queen of the Gaiety Theatre.' After Monckton's death in 1918, this Yorkshire girl of humble origins married the Earl of Dudley.

Grand Theatre shows in the First World War included concerts by and for the Service personnel based round the resort. The programmes of professional shows often carried a panel declaring: 'No members of the cast are eligible for military service.'

Because of the large presence of the Forces, and the resort's sheltered position which continued to attract holidaymakers, the theatre had a profitable war. By the winter of 1916 the Tower Company felt confident enough to keep the theatre open for three weeks after the festive attractions, and made useful money from three excellent shows being toured by Grossmith and Laurillard.

Two were West End successes, *Tonight's The Night,* returning with Jack Buchanan in the cast, and *Potash And Perlumutter,* a Jewish character comedy about two feuding tailors, which had been imported from America.

Most successful of the three January, 1917, shows was *Under Cover,* an American thriller being presented for the first time on a British stage. The star was the handsome Matheson Lang, one of the few straight actors able to attract a good week's business in Blackpool out of season. The play had a clever dramatic twist that took the audience by surprise and it won praise from columnist E.J. Dromgoole in the Gazette. 'It is the kind of play that will attract the theatregoer who is satiated with the unsparkling bubbles of revue and other inconsequential stuff,' he wrote, pointing to the poor quality of some wartime shows.

The Tower Company, he revealed, was having trouble finding suitable shows for the Grand Theatre. Even when they made a good booking, there was a risk of the scenery being lost on the railways, which had become unreliable due to wartime pressures, Dromgoole said. The larger producers had started to duplicate their sets and send them on a week in advance.

The Grand reopened at Easter with one of the biggest successes of the era, the musical comedy *The Maid Of The Mountains,* which was credited with saving Daly's Theatre, and the remnants of the George Edwardes empire, from bankruptcy. After the great producer's death, liabilities of £80,000 emerged. Daly's needed a blockbuster hit to survive.

Singer Robert Evett, after a successful career in musicals, including many Blackpool visits, took over the management and began an urgent search for the crock of gold. He found it in an unproduced script titled *Sheila,* written in 1905 by Frederick Lonsdale, before he became a 'name' writer. The tale was redrafted, scored by Harold Fraser-Simson with lyrics by Harry Graham, and produced on a shoestring by Oscar Asche, with José Collins as the maid, who was renamed Theresa.

After a Christmas, 1916, try-out in Manchester, three songs were added by José's father, J.W. Tate (her mother was variety star Lottie Collins). José had earned £500 a week in New York but for the thinly-financed 'Maid' she reputedly started on £50. Playing opposite Leonard Mackay, as the bandit chief, the role made José one of the most indelibly remembered stars of her time.

The Maid Of The Mountains began its Daly's Theatre run in February, 1917, and was a smash hit. A touring company was immediately formed to cash in on the London success and opened at the Grand, with Frances McLeish and Martin Iredale in the leading roles. The theatre's profit for the week, according to a records book that has survived, was an acceptable £374. The show was rebooked for separate weeks in August and September

Backed by the publicity of a London run that stretched to 1,352 performances, the show made a total of £1,100 for the Grand in two 1918 visits and when José Collins and Leonard Mackay came to the theatre in their original roles in September, 1919, the show broke the box office record. Ticket sales brought in £2,098. After income from the bars and programmes and settlement with the touring company, the Grand made a simple profit of £691.

In spite of the initial success of the musical, the Grand's most popular attraction in 1917 was Gilbert Miller's production of the romantic play *Daddy Long Legs*, by Jean Webster. The story of an orphan girl who fell in love with her mysterious benefactor, it played an August week starring Mary Merrall and her husband, Franklyn Dyall. It gave the theatre a profit of £572 and made good returns for the Grand on several other visits. It became a film and was remade in the Fifties with Fred Astaire and Leslie Caron.

The idea of a repertory season during the usually quiet weeks of early summer was again tried in 1917. It was an admission that the period between the Whitsuntide holiday and the main season was not profitable on a normal weekly change basis. So the management booked Miss Horniman's Manchester repertory company for no fewer than seven weeks, with contemporary plays. The entire venture made only £175 for the theatre.

But the overall results for 1917 were good and the Tower Company decided to keep the Grand open through the winter for the first time in the theatre's history. It was made economical by booking film programmes from late October to Christmas, reducing the risk of losses. For the two-week festive holiday season the company booked a revue, *Zig Zag,* from Moss Empires, and it contributed £546 to profits. According to the surviving records, the Grand Theatre made £6,272 in 1917 — but the revealing fact was that more than half the money came from the seven best weeks of the August-September holiday season.

The following year business was better. A summer holiday boom and a peak in the number of Service personnel convalescing in the Fylde, enabled the theatre to finish with a profit of £11,489. Every show in August and September made more than £500. It was just like the heyday of the George Edwardes musicals.

It was even better in 1919, the theatre making a profit of £12,500, followed by £11,250 in 1920. These figures, from the manager's record books that have survived from the period 1917-1925, show only the simple profit after payment of the visiting companies and settlement of the resident staff's wages, and net income from the bars and programmes. They do not take into account the utility services (modest at that time) or maintenance. But it is fair to assume that by 1920 the Tower Company had recouped the cost of purchase and renovation.

From 1917 to 1920, when business was so good, a few successful shows were booked into the Grand several times. In addition to *The Maid Of The Mountains* and *Daddy Long Legs,* they included the *Bing Boys* series of revues by George Grossmith and Fred Thompson, produced by Grossmith and Laurillard. Most of the music was by Nat D. Ayer and Clifford Grey. Ayer also composed the songs for one of the most popular musical comedies of the day, *Yes Uncle,* which visited the Grand four times and he also brought his variety act to the Blackpool Palace. Another show with four visits was the operetta *The Lilac Domino*, by composer Charles Curvillier and lyricist Harry B. Smith. This was one of the many shows produced by impresario Sir Alfred Butt, whose touring product often came to the Grand Theatre.

Revue gained popularity and two rising names in production, Julian Wylie and James W. Tate, were behind a string of revues that visited the grand. Wylie and Tate built a strong presence in Blackpool, producing summer shows at the Central Pier and, later, the Winter Gardens. Tate and his second wife, singer Clarice Mayne, often appeared at the Palace Varieties.

The box office record set by the *'Maid'* in 1919 was almost equalled by the other musical giant of the time, *Chu Chin Chow,* in the first of its three week visit in August, 1919. This spectacular Arabian Nights-type musical, with music by Frederick Norton, was devised by actor-producer Oscar Asche when he was touring a shortened version of *Kismet* round Northern theatres with his wife, Lily Brayton.

Asche offered his show round the London producing offices and Robert Evett ran it for a month as a fill-in at Daly's. He passed the opinion that it was really a glorified panto and couldn't expect a long West End run. He was correct in one respect. Asche had based the show on *Ali Baba And The Forty Thieves*. The fact that it became such a hit when produced personally by Asche, opening in London in August 1916, was due to its spectacular production values and colourful, but panto-stereotyped, characters.

In five years the show took three million pounds — an unheard of gross in those days — and Oscar Asche personally made £200,000. Together with his fees for staging *The Maid of The Mountains* and other shows for Robert Evett, Mr Asche was for a time the wealthiest actor-producer in the business. But as so often happens in the precarious world of theatrical management, he lost a fortune on an ambitious follow-up to *Chu Chin Chow* (another Eastern piece titled *Cairo)* and had other expensive flops. He left only £20 in 1935.

Sandwiched between the 1919 visit of *Chu Chin Chow* and *The Maid Of The Mountains* was a show that helped launch the American invasion that shook the British musical theatre in the Twenties. The show was *Oh Joy!*, an Anglicised, retitled version of a Broadway hit titled *Oh Boy!*, by the golden partnership of Jerome Kern (music), P.G. Wodehouse (lyrics) and Guy Bolton (libretto). In the West End production the revue star Beatrice Lillie scored her first musical comedy success. The touring version starred Madge White and Guy Grahame.

America had previously had a foot in the door but this time it was serious! As life in Britain returned to normal after the slaughter and hardship of World War One, a new era of social behaviour was shaking off the strictures of Victorian and Edwardian days.

Young Britain welcomed the lively American music. The girls had their hair cut short and their skirts as well. They were ready for a good time. And the Twenties gave them the opportunity.

The lovely Marie Studholme was a Blackpool favourite in musical comedy.

Matheson Lang's Grand Theatre appearances always drew large audiences.

Seymour Hicks and Ellaline Terriss were one of the stage's most popular couples.

CHAPTER SEVEN
The Twenties

BLACKPOOL entertainment companies had a boom in 1920. Balance sheets were healthy; shareholders were happy. New cinemas were opening. And the Tower Company took the decision to refurbish the Grand. They closed the theatre at the end of October for a four-month refit that included the enlargement of the foyer. The company had bought the adjoining gents' outfitters which provided the space for a new, wider staircase to the dress circle and a new cloakroom. The changes to the foyer included marble columns and a balustrade round the 'well' of the dress circle foyer. Marble floors were laid in both upper and lower foyers.

A reporter who described the refurbishment in the Gazette and Herald wrote: 'Inside the theatre the attractive results of the decorator's work is seen on every hand. The new scheme has completely transformed the auditorium. All the old tiled dadoes at the side of the stalls have been renewed, together with the former papering of the walls. The latter are now richly panelled. Lavish use of gold and colour, principally blue, has resulted in a striking change in the appearance of the stage and auditorium.' The article said gold leaf had been used with a lavish hand but the result was tasteful and not garish. Additional lighting had been provided in the form of twin-lamp brackets on the front of the dress circle and upper circle, enhanced by gold silk shades.

The reported noted: 'The dome of the ceiling has had six new panels painted on it. They are charming artistic conceptions. There are two similar paintings on the stage front.' This report suggests that the six ceiling panels of heavenly Cupids date only from 1921 and were applied to match the two panels painted above the proscenium arch during the 1910 refurbishment. The 1921 newspaper report also said the exterior stonework had been cleaned, the distinctive dome had been freshened up with imitation bronze and the upper dome had been re-gilded.

Changes were also evident in the nature of some of the shows coming to the Grand. The American type of revue was so popular in 1920 that it replaced musical comedy for several of the busy summer weeks. Typical titles of these contemporary shows were *The Follies of 1920* and *The Whirl of Today*. When this craze faded the new American musical comedies became established.

There were two prestigious weeks of drama early in the year. The popular Matheson Lang scored a success with his new play *Carnival*, co-written with H.C.M. Hardinge. It was a story of theatrical life set in Venice at carnival time. Lang played a jealous actor whose wife was having an affair. The last act saw the actor trying to murder his wife during a performance of *Othello*.

But the story ended in reconciliation, a romantic device that was good at the box office. Lang opened the play in London the following week. Another big name of the time, Henry Ainlie, brought his production of *Julius Caesar* to the theatre a few weeks later. The local critics admired his Mark Anthony but gave greater praise to the actor playing Cassius. 'A magnificent piece of dramatic art,' said one. The actor was Claude Rains, who was to become one of Hollywood's most cultured leading men.

When *Hobson's Choice,* the Northern comedy by Harold Brighouse, played at the theatre in February, Blackpool turned out in force to see the local actress Maud Banks in the role of Maggie. Her first professional tour in the play, in 1917, had established the actress after her early years with a local amateur company and then with Fred Allandale's Premier Pierrots on the Central Pier.

The most commercially successful show of 1920 at the Grand was a delightful comedy titled *Tilly of Bloomsbury,* by Ian Hay. It was the tale of a middle class girl whose family had fallen on hard times. The parents of her aristocratic fiance were anxious to cast an eye over Tilly's home but it was dowdy and the bills had gone unpaid. On the day of the parents' visit a bailiff arrived with an eviction order but he was persuaded to pose as the unfortunate family's butler, thereby increasing Tilly's marriage chances. Tilly was played by Jane Grahame, popular for her ingenue roles, and the bailiff/butler was Ambrose Manning, whose link with the Grand went back to the 1894 opening week, when he was in Wilson Barrett's company. The provincial premiere of *Tilly of Bloomsbury* was staged at the Grand in July by Grossmith and Laurillard. It gave the theatre a profit of £600 and made several visits over the next two years.

In an effort to rise above the repetitive story lines of English musical comedy, writers were drawing on classic French and English farce for their inspiration. Four examples seen at the Grand in 1920-21 were tour versions of West End successes. With *Who's Hooper?* writer Fred Thompson had borrowed from Arthur Pinero's 1884 legal farce, *In Chancery,* to which songs were added by composers Howard Talbot and Ivor Novello and lyricist Clifford Grey. The touring stars were Jimmy Godden, Evelyn Drew and Bibi Delabere and the show was so successful it was rebooked.

Kissing Time, billed as a musical play by P.G. Wodehouse and Guy Bolton, had been culled from the French farce *Madame et Son Fillene,* by Hannequin and Weber. Music was added by Ivan Caryll. It was a saucy tale about husbands making assignments with the same Parisienne lady! In London, Leslie Henson and Tom Walls starred in the show, which led to their partnership in management and the legendary string of Aldwych farces. Rising stars Norman Griffin and Maidie Andrews headed the touring company in a two-week September visit to the Grand and they were soon teamed again by producer George Grossmith in *A Night Out,* which Grossmith and Fred Thompson had adapted from the Georges Feydeau classic, *Hotel du Libre Echange,* with songs added by

Willy Redstone and Clifford Grey. (The same farce was adapted by Peter Glenville in 1956 as *Hotel Paradiso,* a West End hit for Alec Guinness).

The Blackpool reviewer of the Twenties version enjoyed the romp through the dubious and haunted hotel and an artist's studio and commented that the ladies in the show would not be bothered by the hot weather that had settled on Blackpool! The London production starring Leslie Henson and Stanley Holloway was still running when *A Night Out* first played the Grand at Easter, 1921. The fourth show in this clutch of musical farces was *The Kiss Call,* founded by Fred Thompson on *Le Coup de Telephone,* by Gavault and Berr. The music was provided by Ivan Caryll. There was a strong cast, headed by Stephanie Stephens, Cora Goffin, H.V. Surrey and Tom Shelford.

Blackpool's theatre and cinema owners faced a big rise in wage bills after an agreement negotiated by the theatrical employees' union. It gave increases to box office, front-of-house and stage staff of as much as fourteen shillings a week to senior staff, which indicates how poorly paid they must have been. The Tower Company was reported to be facing an extra wage burden of £20,000 a year.

At a meeting of Blackpool Trades Council a union delegate paid tribute to Alderman W.H. Broadhead, the Blackpool-based theatre magnate and chairman of the pay body, for bringing the two sides to an agreement and giving employees a living wage. Although excellent business cushioned the managements against the increased costs, the boom did not last through 1921. The Armed Forces were no longer in the area to boost the audience figures.

The only show to make big money for the Grand in 1921 was the return visit of *A Night Out,* thanks to the tremendous popularity of Norman Griffin. At Christmas he was back at the theatre in a new musical comedy, *Sally,* a big Broadway success for the writing partnership of Jerome Kern, P.G. Wodehouse and Guy Bolton. In New York Marilyn Miller played the title role; in London it made a star of the American Dorothy Dickson, who settled in Britain. (Her daughter, Dorothy Hyson, married Anthony Quayle). After a successful London launch of the show in September, 1921, George Grossmith quickly sent out a touring company headed by Norman Griffin, Margaret Campbell and Hal Gordon for a Christmas provincial premiere at the Grand Theatre.

The show's Cinderella-type story charmed E.J. Dromgoole, of the Blackpool Gazette and Herald. Reporting that hundreds had been turned away on the opening night, he reeled off an ecstatic review, giving particular mention to a song that was 'cheerful, enlivening, exhilarating.' Millions soon agreed. The song was Jerome Kern's Look *For The Silver Lining.* The show visited the Grand five times in two years.

Almost as successful was the American musical comedy, *Irene,* with music by Harry Tierney and lyrics by Joseph McCarthy. It was yet another variation of the Cinderella tale, with upholsterer's assistant Irene leading a double life in the evenings by modelling the creations of a male couturier known as Madame

Lucy. The first of several Grand theatre visits had Billie Browne as Irene, whose songs included *Alice Blue Gown.*

The British had no reply to this new wave of snappy American shows. So *The Maid of The Mountains* was given an early revival with José Collins in her original part in a tour that did excellent business in a Grand Theatre week in May, 1922. But if English musical comedy was standing still, farce was about to enjoy a boom. The play that is now acknowledged to have led the way was *Tons of Money,* by Will Evans and Valentine. A touring version of this play actually appeared at the Grand in September, 1922, after its success at the Shaftesbury Theatre and before its transfer to the Aldwych where it started the legendary run of farces. It was the first venture in management of Leslie Henson and Tom Walls. Henson later wrote that they had £3 left in the kitty on the opening night. By the time the curtain went up on act two they had sold the American rights for £1,000.

In the November, Matheson Lang came back to the Grand in his new production, *Blood and Sand,* by Tom Cushing from a novel by Blasco Ibanez. It was a macho play about bullfighters and was ideal fodder for Hollywood. But it was not successful on stage and the Blackpool Gazette and Herald reviewer explained why. 'Too much muscle and not enough heart.' He added, pointedly: 'There are periods when an actor of Mr Lang's calibre must realise he is just wasting his time.' The play was certainly spectacular and had a large cast calling for 'doubling' by some members. The reviewer had some fun by reporting: 'The gentleman who figured as Dr Ruiz in the first act and as the Marquis Mornima in the second must have had splendid god-parents, for he is designated Grenville Darling on one occasion and Carlton Love in the next. If he ever takes another part in the play I should not be surprised if his name appears as U.R.A. Dear . . .'

November saw another Jerome Kern hit running in the West End and the Grand was again chosen for the provincial premiere at Christmas. The show was *The Cabaret Girl,* which had been written by George Grossmith and P.G. Wodehouse on a voyage to New York, where they persuaded Kern to write the score. Margaret Campbell and Harold Bradley starred in the initial British tour but by the time of the show's third Grand visit, in September, 1923, Norman Griffin had taken over the male lead.

The Merry Widow, inevitably, came out of retirement in 1923. Grand Theatre audiences saw the revival before it went into Daly's Theatre, London, and had the privilege of seeing the rise of two great stars, the beautiful Evelyn Laye and the handsome Carl Brisson, as Sonia and Danilo. And veteran George Graves had his original 1907 role as Popoff. The show made a week's profit of £400 for the Grand early in March and it proved that operetta still had a firm following.

The choice of Evelyn Laye and Carl Brisson was an indication that a new generation of stars was coming to centre stage. Miss Laye was to have a long association with the Grand and was still carrying off romantic leading roles in her fifties. She was one of a select few artistes whose local appearances were 'musts' with theatregoers. Carl Brisson had a more difficult transition to stardom. The Danish entertainer was touring in a song and dance act with his sister Tilly — indeed, their British debut was in variety at the Blackpool Palace Theatre — when he was signed for *The Merry Widow*. He reputedly had to learn the role parrot-fashion because his English was so weak.

But the former boxer, tall and blonde with a devastating smile, had great charisma. His Blackpool visits until 1940 always set the ladies' hearts fluttering and his showmanship, displayed in impeccable light suits and open cars, caused such fan reaction that he had to live out of town, usually at a Freckleton farm or a caravan at Little Singleton, to avoid the adoring hoardes. He was said to receive up to one hundred love letters a day but his admirers would have been crushed to learn that Brisson was married to a Danish girl, who guided his career. Their son, Freddie, went to Rossall, the public school at Fleetwood, and went on to become an entertainment executive in America. He married the musical comedy star Rosalind Russell.

Another leading man with style and charm was song and dance star Jack Buchanan. He appeared at the Grand in August, 1923, in a Frederick Lonsdale musical play, *Toni,* and was a favourite of the local ladies in his Grand Theatre visits up to 1949.

Along with the revival of *The Merry Widow* came a new Viennese musical, *Lilac Time,* a Drury Lane success that made two visits to the Grand in 1923. Franz Schubert's melodies provided Adrian Ross with a late triumph in his thirty year career as the leading lyric writer for this type of show. It was Ross who wrote the English lyrics for *The Merry Widow* in 1907.

Few shows could be relied on to make money in the theatrical slump of the mid-Twenties. Some Grand Theatre bookings lost money in the summer of 1923 and a Tom Arnold revue, *Better And Better,* did the worst-ever July business, taking a paltry £173 at the box office.

A month earlier an Andre Charlot revue, *Pot Luck,* did at least make a small profit. The stars were Cicely Courtneidge, her husband Jack Hulbert, and Bobby Howes. *Pot Luck* was the show that finally established the Hulberts as a permanent stage and screen couple. After the tour, they and Bobby Howes went into *The Little Revue,* at the Little Theatre, London, and were soon among Britain's biggest stars. All three stars had forty-year associations with the Grand.

On the dramatic side in 1923 and 1924 there were four visits by the legendary Mrs Patrick Campbell, who reprised two famous roles from her early years, *Magda* and *The Second Mrs Tanqueray.* She may have been trading on past glories but three return visits would seem to suggest the theatre management had confidence in the veteran actress.

There was more big-name prestige on the dramatic side in 1924 when Matheson Lang toured in a new play and Sir Frank Benson started a series of annual visits. Sir Frank had been touring for forty years in the plays of

Shakespeare and Goldsmith. He was the only actor to have been knighted in a theatre — by King George V at Drury Lane, in 1916. Now, at sixty-seven, he was nearing the end of his career and had reputedly been grooming Robert Donat to be his successor. But Donat left the company soon after the Blackpool visit and although he occasionally 'guested' with Benson the younger actor obviously saw wider horizons than endless tours in the same old plays. As for Sir Frank, he visited the Grand for several years before he retired.

Perhaps Donat saw himself more in the mould of Matheson Lang, who was cleverly combining careers on stage and screen in subjects of his own choosing. In 1924 he came to the Grand in a political drama titled *The Hour And The Man,* by Frank Stayton. It was an imaginative piece, asking audiences to look into the future of the infant Labour Party. The hero, played by Lang, was Julian Wear, a man of upper class origins who fell on hard times before rising to be a financial journalist and Labour Prime Minister but compromising himself on the way.

A new general manager was in charge at the Grand in 1925. Harry Hall had returned to Blackpool after a period of management in London and had become general manager of the Tower Company's Palace complex, the huge and ornate promenade property that housed a variety theatre, cinema and ballroom. Now he was also given charge of the Grand in a step that was to elevate him to control of all the Blackpool Tower Company's properties.

Hall showed he was not afraid to try new tricks in an attempt to improve theatre business in the mid-Twenties, when cinemas were getting the upper hand. In 1925 he chose the normally slack month of May to experiment with a series of musical comedies on a twice-nightly basis. By reducing the customary long intervals, he was able to fit in two shows, at 6.10 and 8.40pm.

The idea stemmed from the successful introduction of twice-nightly varieties at the Palace Theatre. This was an established practice in the variety world but it was unpopular with artistes in musical theatre, who regarded themselves as rather superior to variety and, in any case, had to work a lot harder and could be on stage for most of a show.

They had nothing to worry about. The experiment failed to produce new patrons. One of the musical comedies that month was *Stop Flirting,* a touring production of the show that had brought Fred and Adele Astaire to London in 1923 for a West End run of four hundred shows. The Astaires did not tour with the show, of course. *Stop Flirting* was the first show seen in Blackpool to have a song by George and Ira Gershwin. The song was *I'll Build a Staircase To Paradise.*

Shocks were in store for some playgoers as a new wave of plays about social problems began to tour. They were far too strong for the Victorian streak in the older generations and were soundly slated by provincial newspaper critics. The first example to arrive in Blackpool was *The Vortex,* which was described by one London writer as 'a dustbin of a play' when it catapulted its author, Noel Coward, to wider fame in 1924. Coward starred in the London production, followed by John Gielgud. The touring version starred George Thirlwell as the drug-addicted Nicky Lancaster and Kate Cutler as his amoral mother. The critic E.J. Dromgoole, of the Blackpool Gazette and Herald, saw it at the Grand in June and he didn't like it. He conceded, however that it was a valid reminder of the horrible results of slighting the laws of decent living.

A year of modest business was saved by the theatre's line-up of big musical shows in the peak August and September holiday weeks. They included two new West End hits, *The Street Singer* and *No No Nanette*. In the first show, which had songs by Harold Fraser-Simson and Harry Graham, the team behind *The Maid Of The Mountains*, Blackpool saw lovely Phyllis Dare as a queen who, in the guise of a street singer, captured the heart of a penniless artist.

No No Nanette was an absolute opposite; a racy show for the Twenties with marital comedy and 'gay young things' in a social whirl. The show's two lasting hits, *Tea For Two* and *I Want To Be Happy,* were well known before the tour reached Blackpool. The musical numbers by composer Vincent Youmans and lyric writers Otto Harbach, Irving Caesar and Frank Mandel, were typical of the fresh new American songs of the thoroughly modern Twenties. Many more would follow from George and Ira Gershwin, Richard Rodgers and Lorenz Hart, and Cole Porter.

No No Nanette made so much money on tour in the United States that it took two years to reach Broadway. By that time it had been exported across the world and the British touring version came to Blackpool only a few weeks after the Broadway opening. In Blackpool it appeared only at the Grand Theatre, with six very successful visits over four years. On the first visit in September, 1925, the Gazette and Herald review began: 'Phew! And again Phew! For a breathless, high speed, roaring, rollicking crescendo of mirth and music...' The stars were Arthur Riscoe (in his first big comedy success) Charles Heslop, Cora Goffin, Maidie Fields and Jessica Bevan.

In July, 1925, Grand audiences saw the highly regarded stage couple Seymour Hicks and Ellaline Terriss, who was making her return to the English stage after a lapse of a few years. The couple had toured Australia before their British tour in *The Man In Dress Clothes,* a French comedy about a man who lost all his possessions except his dress suit. The couple had visited Blackpool for twenty years and the opening night audience gave them a rousing welcome. A reviewer affirmed that Seymour Hicks was 'one of our finest comedy actors.' One month later he was back at the Grand in his own play, *The Price Of Silence,* with Madge Titheradge.

In November, the veteran actor-manager C. Aubrey Smith brought his own production of a West End success, *The Creaking Chair,* which he later took to America and made a new career in Hollywood as the archetypal elderly English gentleman.

The mid-twenties were marked by a shortage of good touring product and

THE PREMIER PLAY HOUSE

GRAND THEATRE

General Manager - GEO. H. HARROP.   Acting Manager - THOS. HOPCUTT.

MONDAY, Sept. 8th, for Six Nights, at 7.30.   MATINEE, SATURDAY, at 2.0.
THE GEORGE EDWARDES Production, under the direction of

ROBERT EVETT,

"THE MAID OF THE MOUNTAINS."

ALL-STAR CAST—

Leonard Mackay, Tom A. Shale, Eric Marshall, William Sarty, Yvonne Phillips, Pauline Chere, and

Miss JOSE COLLINS.

The Play produced by OSCAR ASCHE, producer of "Kismet." Author and producer of "Chu Chin Chow."

SPECIALLY AUGMENTED ORCHESTRA AND FULL CHORUS
Under the direction of J. SHERIDAN GORDON

GRAND THEATRE

General Manager   HARRY HALL

TO-DAY AND WEEK.   SPECIAL MATINEE, SATURDAY, at 2-30.   EVERY EVENING at 7-30.

Personal Visit of

SIR FRANK BENSON

AND HIS COMPANY OF DISTINGUISHED PLAYERS IN PLAYS OF SHAKESPEARE.
OLD ENGLISH COMEDIES AND FAUST

MACBETH | THE RIVALS

THURSDAY.   FRIDAY, Sheridan's Comedy.

SATURDAY MATINEE, at 2-30.   ## AS YOU LIKE IT   SATURDAY MATINEE, at 2-30.

SATURDAY EVENING   ## "FAUST"   The whole Lyceum production by arrangement with the Executors of the late Sir HENRY IRVING

MONDAY NEXT AND WEEK—THE TALK OF LONDON.

ROOKERY NOOK

NOW PLAYING TO CROWDED HOUSES AT THE ALDWYCH THEATRE, LONDON.

MONDAY, 19th November (One Week Only).—For the first time on any British stage.
HERBERT SLEATH and JACK WALLER Present

TALLULAH BANKHEAD

AND THE ORIGINAL SOCIETY, AS PLAYED IN NEW YORK.

THE GOLD DIGGERS

BOX OFFICE NOW OPEN.   'Phone 73.

– Page 62 –

GRAND THEATRE

"BITS AND PIECES"

GEORGE ROBEY

MEWSE & SINGER | HIPPODROME EIGHT
ROBERT LAYTON | PAULA YORK

MARIE BLANCHE

BOOK YOUR SEATS NOW! Phone 73

PERSONAL FAREWELL VISIT OF | ENORMOUS ATTRACTION.

MONDAY NEXT, AND WEEK,

MATHESON LANG

In His Sensational Success

"The CHINESE BUNGALOW"

Prior to his Canadian Tour.

Phone 73.

GRAND THEATRE

MONDAY, May 17th, for TWO WEEKS, at 7.30

HERBERT CLAYTON & JACK WALLER

"NO NO NANETTE"

CHARLES HESLOP   CORA GOFFIN
ARTHUR RISCOE

NOTE.—This is the same cast and production as on our previous visit.

BOOK YOUR SEATS NOW! Phone 73

This and facing page: Local Press advertising of Grand shows in the 1920s the Tower Company's bookers had to plug the gaps in the Grand Theatre schedules with film programmes. But Blackpool already had a dozen well established cinemas and they were the cause of the profit decline at the Grand and other theatres. According to a surviving records book, the Grand ended 1925 with a gross profit of £6,000 — just half the level of the boom years. The first six months of 1925 earned only £1,200 and it would have been even thinner without a sparkling March week of José Collins in a Franz Lehar show, *Frasquita.* It was the star's last musical. After the tour she returned to the variety stage and in August had rave reviews at the Blackpool Palace. In *Frasquita,* Edmund Gwenn had his first musical role and sang with great acceptance, a local reviewer said. The actor later had some fine character parts in Hollywood films.

As Blackpool theatre business began to pick up in 1926, American shows — both plays and musicals — were strongly in evidence. In March the Grand staged the British premiere of *The Best People,* a Broadway success by David Gray and Avery Hopwood. The cast included Olga Lindo, Nora Swinburne, C.V. France and Ian Hunter. In November the Grand also premiered Avery Hopwood's satire on American 'dames' — *The Gold Diggers* — starring Tallulah Bankhead, the expatriate American whose outrageous and eccentric behaviour had made her a darling of London cafe society.

In the summer the Grand had a huge success with the first local visit of the Broadway and West End success, *Rose Marie,* with music by Rudolf Friml and the libretto and lyrics by Oscar Hammerstein 11. It caused an even bigger stir than *No No Nanette* had done the previous year. A show reviewer stressed that it was a musical play with a strong story-line (with a murder) but it was the chorus singing and brilliant dance routines, notably the Totem Dance, that astonished Blackpool audiences. It was a taste of what was to quickly follow in other American musicals. In spite of a heat wave, the theatre was full for two weeks. The title role on this first visit was taken by opera-trained Virginia Perry and Jim Kenyon was played by Jamieson Dodds. In the audience on the opening night was comedy star Billy Merson, who had played Hard Boiled Herman at Drury Lane. His understudy, George Lane, took the role on tour.

No No Nanette made two 1926 visits to the Grand and was making so much money on tour that an earlier Vincent Youmans musical, *Wildflower,* was brought over to cash in on his name. But when it came to the Grand in September, the local management failed to mention the Youmans connection in their advertising. Indeed, the local theatres did little in the mid-Twenties to capitalise on the names behind the American invasion. Shows tended to be marketed on their titles on the basis that they were West End successes. Even the Gershwins, the leading writers of musical shows in the mid and late Twenties, seldom had a mention on theatre showbills and advertisements and their names were often left out of local newspaper reviews of their shows.

Can we assume that these lasting talents were not recognised, at the time, as talents that would last?

Zena Dare returned to the stage in 1926. She had retired at the peak of her fame to marry the Hon. Michael Brett, second son of the second Viscount Esher, in 1911. Sister Phyllis was still starring in musical comedy but Zena resumed her career in light comedy. Her first was the title role in Frederick Lonsdale's *The Last of Mrs Cheyney*, a London success the previous year for Gladys Cooper and Sir Gerald du Maurier. Zena Dare's co-star on tour was Martin Lewis and they appeared before holiday audiences at the Grand in August, 1926.

In the autumn the Grand had no fewer than three of the famous farces produced by Walls and Henson at the Aldwych Theatre. The touring casts were all headed by William Daunt, in the Ralph Lynn 'silly ass' roles, in *Cuckoo In The Nest, It Pays To Advertise* and *Rookery Nook*. Daunt's career had taken a fresh turn in Blackpool four years earlier. After a period with Miss Horniman's Repertory Company at the Gaiety Theatre, Manchester, and the Birmingham Repertory, he had taken a brief Blackpool engagement rehearsing an amateur company. Producer Lionel Bute's tour of *The Sign On The Door* came to the Grand in need of a stage manager. Daunt got the job and within a few months had moved to a similar job at the Aldwych, where he also understudied Ralph Lynn. When the money-spinning Aldwych farces went on tour, Daunt went with them in the Lynn roles.

Another success of 1926 was Matheson Lang's latest tour, in which he played an inscrutable murderer in *The Chinese Bungalow*. Mr Lang told a reporter he had been looking for a suitable Chinese role for twelve years, since his pre-1914 success, Mr Wu. Lang's Grand Theatre appearance was billed as a 'farewell performance' but then a line of small print added 'prior to his Canadian tour.' The actor had been born in Canada, the son of a church minister, but had not visited his native land since the age of six!

Four major musicals totalling eleven weeks were the main strength of the Grand Theatre's 1927 calendar. *No, No, Nanette* played three weeks, *Rose Marie* two weeks, Franz Lehar's *The Blue Mazurka* three separate weeks and the big Gershwin success, *Lady Be Good*, did a week in September and two weeks over Christmas and New Year. This show was the first collaboration of theatre book writers Fred Thompson and Guy Bolton but the story was incidental to the dance music and acclaimed songs of George Gershwin and his lyric-writer brother, Ira. It was their first full musical comedy score.

After the show's success on Broadway, Fred and Adele Astaire brought it to London, where their brilliant dancing and cafe society popularity generated tremendous publicity. George Gershwin also visited London during the West End season. Two well-remembered hits from the show are *Fascinating Rhythm* and *O, Lady Be Good*. After the departure of the Astaires the show went on tour with their roles taken by Annette Mills (sister of John) and husband Robert Seille. Together they had popularised the Charleston dance craze in

Britain. (Twenty years later Annette Mills would win new fame as the presenter of the early television puppet, Muffin the Mule).

The resort was waiting for *Lady Be Good* and the week before its arrival the Gazette and Herald said: *'Lady Be Good* is one of the biggest successes on tour this autumn, doing capacity business everywhere. Its one great factor is that it is always alive and crackles all through . . . with its whirlwind, quickfire dancing.' A local review of the show said the audience had gone with high expectations and had left the theatre full of enthusiasm for 'as bright and merry a production as Blackpool has seen this year.' By coincidence, another Gershwin musical comedy was at the Blackpool Opera House a week later. This was *Tip Toes,* which had played six months in London at the same time as *Lady Be Good.*

All this modern, syncopated music may have been fine for the younger generations. It was the pop music of the day. But the older generations were happy with operetta. One local writer welcomed the now forgotten Franz Lehar show, *The Blue Mazurka,* with the words: 'The growing tendancy of the return to popularity of the more langorous and stately form of musical comedy is emphasised by *The Blue Mazurka* . . . there is absent the breakneck speed to which we have become accustomed by American example.' The show was notable for the appearance of George Metaxa, a minor nobleman who had quit his job with the Romanian Ministry of Agriculture to follow a stage career. A local review noted that he was a tenor of distinction. Two years later Metaxa was starring in the West End in Noel Coward's Viennese musical, *Bitter Sweet.*

Another highlight of 1927 at the Grand was the 'farewell tour' visit of *The Co-optimists,* the famous group of revue artistes. They included founder members Stanley Holloway and Austin Melford. Three months later, Melford was back at the Grand in a musical comedy, *Up With The Lark,* which also starred Britain's leading lady film actress of the day, Betty Balfour. The show followed the August Bank Holiday attraction in which Nellie Wallace, billed as 'the world's most famous comedienne', tried her hand in a musical comedy, *Love And Money,* with songs by R.P. Weston and Bert Lee.

A major upheaval in the local entertainment industry was the talk of the town in 1928. In January a group of shareholders in the Winter Gardens Company invited the Blackpool Tower Company to make an offer for their shares. By May a merger had been signed and sealed. Harry Hall, the Tower Company supremo since the retirement of George H. Harrop, became general manager of the newly designated Blackpool Tower and Winter Gardens Companies. The group took steps to improve their publicity profile and appointed Clem Butson, of the Blackpool Corporation publicity department, to be the firm's first publicity and advertising manager.

Although the Grand Theatre and the Opera House were now under the same management, many of the 1928 bookings had already been made and similar types of shows continued to clash at the two theatres. There were bigger things for the new company to worry about. They faced the dilemma of what to do about talking pictures. With several cinemas on the Fylde Coast, they were hoping, like other operators, that the talkies would be a temporary fad. They certainly had not bargained for the cost of converting their halls for sound, at about £6,000 each. Like most other operators the company decided to wait.

At the Grand in 1928 Gershwin was again the big name in musicals. The theatre's Easter attraction was *Tip Toes,* which had played at the Opera House the previous autumn. The cast was headed by Jean Colin and Reginald Palmer and the score included *That Certain Feeling* and *Sweet and Low Down.* In September the Gershwin brothers' newer show, *Ok Kay!* after Broadway and West End success, was billed at the Grand as a 'colossal attraction'. The stars of the tour were Norah Blaney and Jay Laurier and two great songs stuck in the minds of theatregoers — *Someone To Watch Over Me* and *Do, Do, Do.*

August's holiday attractions included a rare provincial appearance of actor-producer George Grossmith in a Frederick Lonsdale comedy, *Lady Mary.* In the cast was Clifford Heatherley, a Blackpool accountant's clerk who had gained his early stage experience with a local amateur company, the Lyric Players, twenty years earlier and had gone on to spend four years with Beerbohm Tree's company.

The Grand was already well established as a venue for provincial premieres and in 1928 there were two in August. The first was *A Damsel In Distress,* by the prolific comedy writers Ian Hay and P.G. Wodehouse in a 'one off' script. It starred Jane Baxter, Helen Haye, Henry Kendal and Basil Foster. Several years later the show was developed into a romantic screen musical for Fred Astaire. The second premiere was of a romantic musical *The White Camelia,* which starred Hary Welchman.

Matheson Lang made one of his popular Grand appearances in a well-crafted political thriller, *Such Men Are Dangerous,* adapted from the German by Ashely Dukes. In the cast was an actor making a name for himself: Donald Wolfit. Thrillers of a more commercial slant seemed to be on tour by the dozen. They were quaintly referred to as 'crook plays' and those with ghostly goings on were 'spook and crook plays'. Sinister deeds developed under atmospheric lighting as the professional theatre responded to the impending arrival of talking pictures by trying to frighten the wits out of patrons. Many of the 'crook plays' were adapted by Edgar Wallace from his popular crime novels. He was one of the few writers to see his name given the same advertising weight as his titles.

Early in 1929 the local theatre and cinema owners faced the news they had been dreading. One of the companies was equipping for the talkies. The owners of the Princess and Hippodrome cinemas sold out to Associated British Cinemas, who were assembling a nationwide chain and at Easter the Hippodrome screened Blackpool's first talkie, Al Jolson in *The Singing Fool,* with four separate shows each day. There was still a belief among some owners that sound films would not last. Even the mighty Tower and Winter Gardens Companies would only risk converting one hall, the Winter Gardens Pavilion, which joined the sound revolution in May with matinee-only film shows. The summer stage show had already been contracted for evening performances.

In April the Grand had a wonderful week's business from the 'stupendous attraction' of Gracie Fields starring in *The Show's The Thing,* a show written and produced by her husband, Archie Pitt, immediately prior to opening at London's Victoria Palace. Gracie received possibly the greatest write-up of any star who had appeared at the Grand Theatre up to that time. A Gazette and Herald reviewer wrote: 'What a reception they gave her . . . Miss Fields responded by proving herself better than ever; a brilliant, versatile artiste, a fine singer, a clever actress, a marvellous mimic and, above all, possessed of the rarest of gifts — the gift that has made Chaplin supreme in another sphere — the power to stir an audience to the very depth of emotion one minute and to make it hold its sides in uncontrollable mirth the next.' The writer noted that Gracie had become an international star since her last Blackpool appearance, at the Palace Varieties in December, 1927. He added: 'During the last twelve months no artiste has been so prominent and persistently before the public. Miss Fields's success may have astonished some of her critics but her native Lancashire was not the least surprised.'

The two most talked-about plays of the year appeared at the Grand in 1929. In the spring, Frank Lawton repeated the London role that sealed his stardom, as *Young Woodley,* the public school boy who fell in love with his house-master's wife in John Van Druten's world-wide hit. The 'scandalous' thing was that the wife responded. A fine cast included Molly Rankin, Henry Mollison and Basil Langton in the Basil Dean production. In the autumn, R.C. Sherriff's war play, *Journey's End,* made an even stronger impact because its ultimate message was (unpatriotically) the futility of war.

Perhaps for this reason, the play had been passed over by the major London producing companies and it was left to Maurice Browne, a pioneer of the American little theatre (repertory) system to produce it in London and New York, to great acclaim. Reaction in London was so controversial (with the brilliant young Laurence Olivier as Captain Stanhope) that the job of reviewing it in Blackpool's newly-launched Evening Gazette was taken on by the editor, Harold R. Grime, under his by-line H.R.G., who had served in the Army in France during World War One. He wrote that the play, set in a trench on the Western Front had become an anti-war sermon by accident. By design it was a drama of the front line with great suspense woven with humour. Indeed, it had more humour than the average farce, he said. It was portrayed so realistically 'that some of us would not have been surprised to see a large, sleek, corpse-fed rat waddling across the footlights'. He praised the uniformly high level of performance and said it would be invidious to single out particular members of the company. So he didn't. Readers had to wait for the weekend show column to see the list of players, who were led by Cyril Gardiner, as Stanhope.

Among the regular attractions transferred from the Opera House to the Grand Theatre in 1929, under the Tower Company's merger rationalisation, was actor-manager Hamilton Deane, who specialised in thrillers and chillers. His two-week spring visit included his three most famous roles — *Bulldog Drummond, Dracula* and (Baron) *Frankenstein.*

At the height of the summer season the Grand had a two-week run of *Mr Cinders,* a musical comedy that had been premiered by producer Julian Wylie at the Blackpool Opera House, with Binnie Hale and Bobby Howes heading the cast, a year earlier. It became a West End hit and started to tour with Margery Wyn and Hindle Edgar in the leading roles. Mr Cinders, remembered mainly for the Vivian Ellis song, *Spread A Little Happiness*, was revived in the West End in the Eighties and played three weeks at the Grand in the 1984-85 festive season.

The Twenties ended in gloom for theatres. Talking pictures caught on in a big way. Repertory companies sprang up everywhere in a bid to cut the costs of touring theatre — and keep the producers in business. Blackpool had no fewer than five repertory companies towards the end of 1929. Even the Tower Circus had a resident 'rep' after the summer season, playing on a stage built across one of the entrances to the circus ring.

At the Grand Theatre, rising young impresario Barry O'Brien had the best local company. Three 'names' in his cast were June Lewis-Walker, George Bishop and Ennis Lawson and he ran a ten-week season from early November, with a policy of famous contemporary plays. It can't have been plain sailing because the name of the company changed three times. It started as the Blackpool Repertory Players, became the Barry O'Brien Players and ended up as Barry O'Brien's West End Company.

It was apparently a stop-gap measure for the Tower Company management for important decisions had to be made about the future of the Grand Theatre as 'the talkies' took an ever larger share of audiences in the new year.

SELECTIVE INDEX — Personalities

Selective Index of Shows